About the Author

◇◇◇◇◇◇◇◇◇◇◇◇◇◇◇◇◇◇◇◇

Sourabh Mukherjee is the author of bestselling books *The Highway Murders, Death Served Cold, The Trail of Blood, The Sinners* and *In the Shadows of Death*. He has also written three short story collections and bestselling books in Bengali, as well as a popular textbook. He has written columns for Sportskeeda and Yahoo! Sports.

India Today has honoured him as one of the "ten celebrated role models of 2022" and *Outlook* calls him one of the "top ten personalities to look upon if you are looking for an inspiration".

Sourabh speaks regularly in book fairs and literary events in different parts of India. He has won several literary awards and recognitions, some of the recent ones including Hall of Fame in Literoma International Symposium for Literature and Festival (2020), and Guest Speaker in Oxford Bookstores Online Festival (2020). He was awarded the Man of Excellence Award, 2021 by Indian Achievers' Forum for his professional achievements and contributions to nation-building.

An Electronics and Telecommunications Engineer from Jadavpur University, Kolkata, in his day-job, Sourabh works in a senior leadership role in a global technology firm. He has spoken in global technology summits in London and Las Vegas, as well as at events organized by Society for Data Science, Bengal Chamber of Commerce and Industry, IIT, IIM, IIFT, Symbiosis, St. Xavier's University, Kolkata University, IISWBM, Techno India, and University of Engineering & Management among many others.

Website: www.sourabhmukherjee.com
Facebook: authorsourabhmukherjee
Instagram: authorsourabhmukherjee
Twitter: sourabhm_ofcl

Other books by the author

Appreciation for the author and his works

◇◇◇◇◇◇◇◇◇◇◇◇◇◇◇◇◇◇◇◇◇◇◇◇

"Sourabh Mukherjee has emerged as one of the front-runners in Indian crime fiction over the last five years."

—Mid-day

"Mukherjee has left his mark on the genre."

—Deccan Herald

"One of the most popular writers of Indian crime fiction."

— The Asian Age

"Death Served Cold is a compelling read based on true events."

— The Times of India

"In Death Served Cold, the author explores the dark recesses of the female psyche."

— IANS

"Death Served Cold reveals shocking excesses of sadism and aggression rarely associated with women."

— Lokmat Time

"The Sinners is a thrilling work of fiction that weaves together elements of corporate warfare and personal vendetta."

— Yahoo News

"The Sinners is definitely the must–read thriller book of the year."

— The Week

"The Sinners is a gripping and riveting read."

— Outlook

"Set in the city of Kolkata, In the Shadows of Death is a fast-paced potboiler which hooks you and keeps you glued to the plot from the very beginning."

– The Times of India

"With an almost Freudian understanding of how our childhood experiences influence our adult decisions, Sourabh's novel (In the Shadows of Death) paints a stark picture of urban life in India."

– The Hindu

"The theatrical finale comes as much from the extraordinary storytelling as it does from the reveal of the murderer. Mukherjee has the unerring eye of a master craftsman."

– The Hindu

"Just when you think you've got it all figured out as per the clues that the killer leaves like crumbs, the author throws you off the path repeatedly with the twists."

–The News Now

"A whodunit with several twists, In the Shadows of Death has elements of romance, corporate scandals, and suspense with a strong emotional undercurrent."

– The New Indian Express

"A heady concoction of thrill, mystery, psychology and humanity is what makes this book (In the Shadows of Death) such an engrossing fare."

– Punjab Tribune

"In the Shadows of Death is crisp, well-composed and there are no loose ends to irk your mind."

– Yahoo News

"In the Shadows of Death is a page turner till the

end with its fluid narrative infused with twists and revelations, which constantly raise your curiosity level."

– Zee News

"A psychological thriller in the true sense of the phrase, In the Shadows of Death delves deep into the psyche of its characters."

– The Free Press Journal

"The character of detective Agni Mitra has been rendered in a very believable and realistic fashion. The author has rummaged into the human psyche and used it as the basis for the detective's theories."

– Tahlka News

"The novel (In the Shadows of Death) explores the city of Kolkata in a way few contemporary novels have attempted. The City of Joy is not just a backdrop but another character in the novel."

– Go–Getter, Go Air in-flight magazine

THE WEB OF LIES

A DETECTIVE AGNI MITRA NOVEL

SOURABH MUKHERJEE

Srishti
PUBLISHERS & DISTRIBUTORS

Srishti Publishers & Distributors
A unit of AJR Publishing LLP
212A, Peacock Lane
Shahpur Jat, New Delhi – 110 049

editorial@srishtipublishers.com

First published by
Srishti Publishers & Distributors in 2023

10 9 8 7 6 5 4 3 2 1

This is a work of fiction. The characters, places, organisations and events described in this book are either a work of the author's imagination or have been used fictitiously. Any resemblance to people, living or dead, places, events, communities or organisations is purely coincidental.

The author asserts the moral right to be identified as the author of this work.

Printed and bound in India

To Ma and Baba
This space is too small for the 'why's.

Chapter 1

When Manav opened his eyes, he realized that he was lying on a patch of grass by the road. He might have been briefly unconscious. Blood trickled down his neck from under his ear. He had been hit, extremely hard, repeatedly. He could feel a searing pain in his head.

His face was contorted in pain. Blood poured from the wound in his head, streamed past his jaw forming rivulets that landed on his shirt. One of his nostrils was clogged with blood and he had difficulty breathing. He wanted to cry for help. His swollen lips moved, but his voice failed him. He tasted blood in his mouth. His outstretched hands grabbed the cold air of the night.

There were tears flooding out of his eyes from the pain. He could barely open them. Through the narrow slits that his eyes had been reduced to, he could see blurred images of the three men dragging his wife away like a rag doll along the dusty road. He could see her flailing hands. Her helpless cries seemed to float in from a distant planet. Something had happened to his eyesight. She was going in and out of focus. The blood was fast spreading around his neck.

He turned his head and looked at their car which was parked a few feet away. The three men had shattered the windows. He could see his chauffeur, slouched at the wheel. Was he still alive?

He mustered the last vestiges of his strength and tried to crawl on his elbows and knees. He had not progressed even a few inches before he gave in to the excruciating pain. The minutes passed and Manav lay where he was, unmoving.

***

The breeze of the night felt cold on his bare torso as Mushtaq walked out of the makeshift car garage, zipping up his trousers. Running his fingers through his grubby hair, he turned back.

He could see Rishi tottering out of the garage. Ashfaq was still at it, his hips moving back and forth between the outstretched legs of the woman, his throaty groans feeling the stifled air of the dingy garage. The woman lay still under him.

'Enough! She must be dead by now!' Mushtaq said, laughing. He was joined by Rishi. 'Relieve yourself and slit her neck, you horny bastard. We need to get the hell out of here, fast! It's clearing up,' Mushtaq added, as he looked at the dull grey sky. The two men made their way towards the bike parked outside the garage.

Ashfaq finally ejaculated inside the motionless woman with a grunt. He wiped the sweat off his brow and looked around for the dagger he had been carrying in the small of his back. He remembered throwing it away carelessly when he had unbuckled his belt and lowered his pants before he pounced on the woman.

He found it lying a few inches away and picked it up. The edge of the knife had all but grazed the edge of the woman's neck when Ashfaq suddenly stopped, as if he had remembered something.

He looked around, making sure the others were not watching. Those idiots had no appreciation for his romantic fancies. They did not call him *Rangeela* without a reason.

He pulled out his mobile phone and turned on the camera.

He lay down next to the woman, his sweat-slicked cheek rubbing against hers, and held the phone a few inches above their faces. Her hair was matted in sweat, the eyes had been reduced to tiny white slits, the mouth was gaping, her lips and cheeks were bruised, and her face had a deathly pallor.

Ashfaq smiled at the camera and clicked.

After all, it was not every day that one managed to click a picture lying next to Hiya Sen, the heartthrob of millions. That too, her last picture ever!

Chapter 2

'A Macallan with three ice, if you have the time,' Agni rolled his eyes in exasperation as he repeated his order at the bar.

Joseph flashed a sheepish grin. He had been busy showing off his cocktail mixing skills to a group of giggling college girls at the bar.

'I have all the time for you, sir,' he said apologetically, still smiling.

'I have no doubt about your mixing skills,' Agni gestured at his cocktail flask, 'but you are a pathetic liar.'

A live band was serenading the weekend crowd with one love song after another. Agni looked around and noted how the same song evoked different reactions among different people. The lovers were lost in each other's eyes, oblivious to the world around them. Single men and women were bestowed with renewed optimism about love. Those who had recently broken up with their loved ones got teary-eyed, reached for their phones in a drunken stupor and started typing out messages they would invariably regret in moments of sobriety the next morning. Agni smiled to himself. He did not fit into any of those categories, and he did not complain.

As he finished his third and was about to order the next, Agni was conscious of a sudden hubbub around him. There was palpable excitement in the air which seemed to have taken over the lazy romanticism of the ambience.

Agni turned around and the reason for that radical mood shift among the guests in the bar was right there in front of his eyes. Rituja Bose had just stepped into the bar. Rituja had been ruling the Tollywood silver screen for close to two decades and had made as many headlines for her box office successes as for her scandalous escapades. She walked across the bar ignoring sighs, lusty gazes and envious glances like only celebrities of her stature could, stopping only now and then to wave and flash plastic smiles at a few equally famous socialites.

Now a middle-aged woman, she filled out her black sequined evening dress that accentuated her curves. Her hair was tied back in a bun and the makeup was loud. Members of the staff competed with each other to make her comfortable. It was, however, the manager, who finally had the privilege of escorting Rituja to her seat at the far corner of the bar.

Rituja untied her hair and lit a cigarette. Blowing out, she closed her eyes and threw her head back. When she opened her eyes again, they landed on Agni.

He had been watching her intently. Agni wondered if Rituja Bose remembered him. Several years had passed though. Almost a decade now.

Did he see a faint remembrance flash across those eyes? Did those crimson lips curve just a wee bit in a smile? Was there a slight lift of the wine glass in acknowledgement of the presence of the celebrity cop? Or was Agni's mind playing tricks, making him see things he wanted to see?

His phone buzzed. It was a message from the Commissioner. *We will need your help in the Hiya Sen case.*

Chapter 3

Inspector Arya pushed the cup of black coffee towards Agni. He had taken up charge of the New Town police station sometime back.

'The worst part of being in charge of a high-profile case is the constant media glare. Everyone seems to have an opinion,' Arya complained.

'Arya, let's not forget we are talking about Hiya Sen here. She was a youth icon. Her last few movies struck gold at the box office, and I read in a tabloid the other day that there were rumours that a big production house in Mumbai had approached her weeks before her tragic death for a role in their next project. And let's also not forget who she was with. I feel Manav Chauhan is not just the scion of a famous industrialist family, but, over the last few years, he has carved out a distinct identity for himself as one of the key architects of the new face of this city, building one plush mall and residential complex after another. Their wedding made headlines for a week!

'And then, you have the darling of the city brutally raped and murdered in less than a fortnight after her wedding, and the business magnate is still fighting for his life in a hospital. And whether you like it or not, you are the one who is out to nab the bastards who brought this upon our city. How can you shy away from the flash bulbs, my friend?' Agni smiled.

He took a sip of the coffee and added, 'But I have to say you have handled it very well so far, Arya. After all, you have those three men behind bars already. Which makes me curious...' Agni paused briefly and then said, 'what made you reach out for my help? I thought you had it all wrapped up!'

Agni had been informed by the Commissioner that it was Arya who had put in a special request for Agni's attention to the case.

'Not quite, Agni, not quite,' Arya sighed, 'a few interesting details came to light when we questioned those three men.'

'We'll come to that. I know a lot about this case from the relentless media coverage over the last few days. But, it still won't hurt to hear all about it from you. Let's begin from the start.' Agni reclined in his chair, as Arya cleared his throat.

'Manav and Hiya were partying that night in a club close to the airport. Manav had an argument with these three men inside the club. They had reportedly misbehaved with Hiya.'

'They were at Tipple, I assume?' Agni asked, referring to the club close to the Netaji Subhas Chandra Bose International Airport, which had come up a few months back and had in no time, turned into the destination of choice for the rich and the famous in the city.

'You are right.'

Agni's attention was again focused on Arya's account.

'Do we have eyewitnesses to the brawl?'

'Yes. Quite a few, actually.'

'Carry on...'

'When Manav left the club with his wife in his car, the three men followed them. The car was stopped in New Town. It was heavily damaged. Manav and his chauffeur were beaten up and Hiya was dragged to a nearby garage where she was gang-raped and then, had her throat slit.'

'Who reported the incident?' Agni asked next.

'A police patrol car found Manav's car by the road. The chauffeur was inside the car. Manav was found a short distance away from the vehicle. Both of them were unconscious and had sustained grievous injuries. They were taken to the nearest private hospital on the Eastern Metropolitan Bypass. When we informed the family, we learnt that Manav and Hiya had gone out together that night. I sent out my men immediately to look for Hiya. Within a couple of hours, we found her inside that garage. It was not too far from where the car had been found.'

'What about those three men? Mushtaq, Rishi and Ashfaq – right?' Agni checked if he had the right names. Arya nodded in affirmation.

'How did you find them?' Agni asked.

'We made their sketches based on Manav's descriptions. We scanned the CCTV footages at Tipple. We spoke to the waiters and the bartender. Apparently, they were regulars there. The kind that has come into easy money by crooked means, spending all they earn on liquor and women. Probably henchmen of some mafia boss. It wasn't too difficult to nab them. In fact, one of them had shot a selfie with Hiya.' Arya smiled.

'Are you serious?' Agni said.

'Yes, he said he couldn't bring himself to delete it from his phone. The others were not aware of this. But you must see their attitude! They feel they own this city, just because they carry guns and have a few political and mafia connections. Makes me sick!'

'Well, incidents of crime never turn out to be as simple as they tend to look on the surface, do they?' There were wrinkles on Agni's brow.

'I made a list of people you may want to talk to,' Arya produced a sheet of paper and placed it on the table. Having spent close to a couple of years with Agni, Arya was beginning to get familiar with his modus operandi.

'You seem to have everything figured out,' Agni smiled, reminding himself one more time why he loved working with the man sitting across the table.

'But first things first. When can I talk to those three men you arrested?'

Chapter 4

Mushtaq, Rishi and Ashfaq looked at each other.

The man sitting in front of them was very different from the other cops who had been interrogating them all these days. This one did not use force. He never raised his voice. He never lost his composure. But his eyes were intimidating. It seemed as if they reached the deepest recesses of their minds.

'So, who were you after? Manav Chauhan or Hiya Sen?' Agni transferred a paperweight from one hand to the other, his eyes sweeping across the faces of the three men sitting across the table.

None of them spoke.

Agni bent forward. 'This is not helping. I asked you who your target was.'

Ashfaq looked up and glared menacingly at Mushtaq.

'*You* led the operation. Why don't *you* answer him? You are the one who got all of us into this!'

'Take it easy, tiger!' Agni dissuaded Ashfaq, who seemed ready to pounce on Mushtaq.

Ashfaq hid his face in his palms and started howling. 'I don't believe I did that to Hiya! I gave in to my greed, sir. I never missed any of her movies.' He touched his heart. 'I'm her biggest fan, sir. And I did *that* to her...'

Agni turned towards Mushtaq. 'What do you have to say? Looks like you were the mastermind!'

'Asif *bhai* promised a lot of money, sir,' Mushtaq muttered, not looking at Agni. 'And now, we're screwed!'

'Who is Asif bhai?'

'Asif bhai takes contracts sir, and we do the dirty work. We don't ask him questions. He got us a number of jobs in the past and the money was always good.'

'Would Asif bhai not know who paid him?'

'He might. We have no idea.' Mushtaq pleaded.

'Where is he now?' asked Arya.

'No trace of Asif bhai, sir. That's what we heard...' Mushtaq turned towards Arya. He looked crestfallen. 'We work for him, sir. He said he would make sure we were out of town the very next day. Instead, he himself went into hiding. And we landed up here! The police don't seem to have any idea who paid him for the job.'

'Why don't you answer my first question then? The situation can't get any worse for the three of you, can it? Who were you after—Hiya or Manav?'

'Do we have to say this in the court, too?' Mushtaq sounded apprehensive.

'It's entirely up to you,' Agni leaned back in his chair.

'Our target was... H...Hiya,' Mushtaq sounded hesitant. The three men could not figure out what the cop was up to.

'What about Manav Chauhan and his driver?'

The three men looked at each other. 'They resisted us, sir.'

'And you beat them up!' Agni completed the thread for Mushtaq.

'When did you last meet Asif bhai?' Agni asked next.

'The day before the operation, sir. We had no idea he had been planning to leave the country. He had never gone into hiding in the past, sir. We don't know why he fled this time!' Rishi finally spoke, unbridled rage writ large on his face. His eyes burnt like embers.

'He still owes you some money, I assume,' Agni smiled.

'Of course, he does,' Rishi thumped on the arm of his chair. 'That bastard!'

'You better get a good lawyer,' Agni stood up and signalled at the constable to take the three men away.

As they were being taken away, Agni could hear Ashfaq still muttering, 'I don't believe I slit her throat...'

'Very interesting, indeed!' Agni smiled and turned towards Arya.

'Agni, when we questioned them earlier, they kept saying that they had been paid for the job,' Arya said.

'I wouldn't be surprised. That, in my opinion, seems to be the livelihood of these boys. I believe that they really don't know where the money trail started from. Did we look for this... Asif bhai?' Agni asked further.

'We checked on his whereabouts based on the information we gathered from the three of them. Asif bhai operated from a slum in Tiljala. He would normally take contracts over phone and the money would be transferred to anonymous bank accounts. He would then engage his boys to execute the contracts. They were not supposed to ask any question. It seems Asif bhai fled the country before the incident, probably with a forged passport. We are yet to track him down. We have now got in touch with Interpol.' Arya answered.

Agni nodded. He was lost in his thoughts. After a few minutes, he asked, 'Don't you find it odd that these three men were overexposed and almost courted arrest?'

'Yes—they keep saying that Asif bhai had assured them that they would be out of town the very next day.'

'But the reality was quite different, wasn't it? They were almost handed over to you on a platter!' Agni muttered, without looking at Arya. He spoke after a while. 'So, the money trail has effectively dried up.'

Arya said, 'It has, unfortunately. We have a watertight case against these three men, with motive as well as opportunity. That will be good enough to get closure on this case for the media and the public. The conspiracy theorists can, of course, go on speculating. But, for my peace of mind, I want to trace the alleged money trail to its origin.'

'This case involves the who's who of the city, Arya. The Commissioner tells me that the media is watching every single move we make. The Chief Minister herself has been asking for daily updates.'

'Let's see if we can get to the bottom of this. We need to figure out very quickly, who wanted to harm the couple, and hired Asif bhai for the job. Assuming, of course, that those three men are speaking the truth. Otherwise, we have a foolproof case against them, and we can conveniently follow that line of investigation,' Arya said.

Chapter 5

As Agni drove through the rush hour traffic with Arya for company, he soaked in the festive spirit in the air. With Durga Puja around the corner, there were frenzied activities all over Kolkata. Clubs in every locality were gearing up for the biggest festival of the year, going around collecting donations from households in the neighbourhood. Narrow lanes of the city were blocked off to accommodate the *pandals*, which were being built over several weeks. Most of those lanes would remain out of bounds for vehicles for weeks after Durga Puja, well past Diwali. All through his drive, Agni had to take long detours along congested roads.

Decorators commissioned from faraway towns like Chandannagar, were busy setting up elaborate lighting arrangements inside the pandals and lining the roads leading up to them. With several corporate and media houses introducing awards in a variety of categories over the last few years, a spirit of healthy competition had been infused into puja arrangements in Kolkata. The height of the idol, the theme of the pandal, lighting and interior decorations, environment friendliness, community spirit—there was a prize up for grabs for every aspect of the festivities.

The artisans were busy giving finishing touches to the idols in their workshops in Patuapara and Kumortuli. Enthusiasts across the city thronged to these workshops to watch the clay idols come to life with impeccable strokes of the brush. The roads were already overflowing with people going around shopping for the grand festival.

When Agni finally reached the private hospital on the Eastern Metropolitan Bypass where Manav Chauhan and his driver Lakhan Sahu had been admitted, it was well past noon. Lakhan was at the wheel of the car in which Manav and Hiya were returning home from the club on that fateful night.

As they walked into the hospital, the stark contrast with the general air of mirth outside was conspicuous. There were patients being carried around in gurneys, relatives waited anxiously in the lobby, the air was heavy with the smell of sickness, and everyone seemed to be in a hurry.

Agni and Arya were directed to a room on the first floor.

'I must say that the Chauhans have been very kind to their chauffeur, paying for his treatment in a single-occupancy cabin in an expensive private hospital,' Arya remarked as they stepped out of the elevator.

'So it seems,' smiled Agni.

Entering the room, they saw an emaciated man on the bed, his bandages leaving very little of his face discernible.

Agni and Arya introduced themselves. Conscious of the constraint on time, Agni came straight to the point.

'Lakhan, can you tell us what exactly happened that night when you were returning from the club?'

Agni listened intently as Lakhan recounted the incidents of the night, speaking almost in whispers.

'We were in New Town. The roads were empty – no pedestrian in sight, hardly any traffic at that time of the night. A bike with three men stormed past our car out of the blue, and blocked our way, making a turn along the width of the road. I pressed the brakes with all my strength to avoid running into the bike. By that time, they had stepped down and started walking towards our car. Two of them were carrying iron rods. Before we realized what was going on, they started smashing the windows. One of them reached inside the car and hit me on the head with a rod. Everything around me was reduced to a blur. I passed out.'

'You remember nothing of what happened after that, I assume?'

'No, sir. When I woke up, I was in the hospital.' Lakhan wept silently. 'I came to know the next morning. The horrible things they did to Hiya *bitiya*. *Chhote malik* was also beaten up, I heard.'

'Didn't you see the bike following you all the way from the club? Weren't you suspicious at any point in time?'

'Sir, on the Eastern Metropolitan Bypass, there were a number of cars and bikes. There was no reason to be suspicious. Thereafter, when I was driving through New Town, it was quite late and I was concentrating on the road ahead. I did notice the bike behind us, but I never suspected anything.'

Agni had more questions, but they were interrupted by the nurse walking into the room. 'I'm sorry, sir, but your time is up. It's lunch time,' she announced with a tone of authority.

Agni looked at his watch and gestured to Arya. It was time to leave. He thanked Lakhan and walked out.

When they came out into the lobby, Agni looked at Arya and asked, 'How do you think it went? Anything struck you as odd?'

'The same story. I didn't hear anything we didn't know already.' Arya looked somewhat disappointed.

'Well, I cannot put my finger on it, but something didn't sound right,' Agni's brows were creased. Arya failed to understand why.

Agni looked at his watch and said, 'We have some time before we get to meet Mr Chauhan. Let's get some lunch.'

The two men headed for the cafeteria inside the hospital.

Chapter 6

The man who greeted Agni and Arya with a feeble smile and gestured to a sofa set adjacent to his bed had graced countless magazine covers over the last couple of years. He had a bandage across his forehead, and his right arm was in a plaster cast. So were his legs under the bedsheet. The injuries that were not visible to the naked eye included three broken ribs and a linear fracture to the skull. His eyes still had not cleared up. The doctor had said that it was a condition fairly common after a head injury. He had also warned that the damage might be permanent. He would be keeping a close watch.

His hair was dishevelled with a few strands across the bandage on his brow. His stubble was a few days old, and his sharp nose and cheek bones seemed to have been accentuated further by the general frailty of his face. His large brown eyes had none of the confident shine with which he stared into the eyes of the reader from the pages of business and lifestyle magazines, tabloids and newspapers every other day. The white shirt of the hospital uniform, however, strained against his broad chest and his sculpted biceps which reminded one of the rigorous exercise routines that Manav Chauhan famously subjected himself to, every day of the week.

The doctor in charge had warned Agni that although his physical wounds were healing fast, Manav was yet to recover completely from the intense trauma that the incident had caused.

Agni, therefore, had to exercise caution while speaking to Manav and make sure that he did not dwell on the incidents of the night.

After the exchange of pleasantries, Agni said, 'Mr Chauhan, I know you have already spoken to the police. You must also be aware of the fact that the miscreants are now in custody. I have been requested by the Commissioner of Police to look into, let's say, a few irregularities in the statements of the three men who have been arrested. This won't take too long, I promise.'

'Go ahead, ACP Mitra. It doesn't matter, really. Those scenes keep haunting me every time I close my eyes, in any case. Your asking me a few questions will not make it any worse. It must be the doctor who has warned you!' Manav smiled.

'Thanks, Mr Chauhan, I will not waste any more of your precious time,' Agni came straight to the point. 'Your fairy tale wedding to the late Ms Sen took everyone by surprise. How long had the two of you known each other?'

Arya noticed a dry smile flash across Manav's face.

'It was, what they call, a whirlwind romance. We met during an event in one of my properties in South Kolkata. She had been invited as one of the guests of honour. We warmed up to each other rather easily. She was not just a very beautiful woman. She had a great personality, she was a whole lot of fun, she was kind and most importantly, she listened to her heart and spoke her mind. How many of us can do that? And, unlike most people around me, she was not intimidated by my authority. I found that refreshingly different. I realized she was the woman who would keep me grounded.' Manav paused and let out a deep sigh.

He looked away from the policemen and said, 'But that was not to be.'

He quickly gathered himself and smiled at Agni, 'Can you believe it? She was the one who asked me out on our first date! I had just broken up with my fiancée and had not been too sure about getting into another relationship. But Hiya swept me off my feet. We decided to get married within two months!'

'Destiny always has its way, doesn't it?' Agni had a wry smile on his lips. 'It had been less than a fortnight after your wedding, right?' he asked Manav.

'Let me see,' Manav paused briefly and then said, 'Twelve days to be precise. Hiya wanted to go on a honeymoon, but I was the one who suggested we go later as I had a few business meetings lined up here in Kolkata. I wish I had listened to her and taken her somewhere far from the city!'

'If I may ask you about the events of that fateful night, what happened inside Tipple?' Agni asked, his voice betraying the caution he subjected himself to.

Manav closed his eyes for a moment, as if to get his thoughts together. Arya saw fleeting glimpses of pain across that heavily bruised face.

When he opened his eyes again, Manav looked at Agni and said, 'Those three men, the ones you now have in your custody, had been drinking heavily and started misbehaving with Hiya on the dance floor. As you will understand, being an actress, Hiya was used to public attention and overenthusiastic fans. There had been instances in the past when an odd fan had crossed limits and Hiya had handled such situations with courage and grace. However, that evening, those three men crossed all limits of decency. They were coming on to her with lewd remarks and gestures. That was when I lost my calm. We had a heated argument. Blows were exchanged, though I am sure you would understand that I am not the sort of person who would normally get into a bar brawl. But then, it was not destined to be your regular night, was it?' Manav shifted painfully on the bed. He looked outside the window. It was a dull grey autumn afternoon. Manav saw the trees tossing their heads in the breeze, their leaves beginning to turn yellow. There was an air of melancholy in the room even as the city outside geared up for festivities.

He said almost in whispers, 'The games our destiny plays with us! Maybe I should have ignored those bastards that night, after all.'

Everyone in the room went quiet. Arya realized Manav Chauhan's life had been reduced to one of endless regrets.

Agni broke the silence after a while.

'While you were on your way home, you never noticed the bike following your car?'

'No, we did not pay attention.'

'I believe Lakhan was attacked first.'

'He was,' Manav closed his eyes again. 'He is still in this hospital.'

'Yes, we met him some time back. He is getting better, as I was told.'

'He has been with me for more than five years now. He is like family.'

'I understand.' Agni paused for a while and continued, 'Mr Chauhan, when you saw Lakhan taking the blow, didn't you call someone for help? Of course, it must have been too unexpected, and you might not have had the time to react.'

'You are right, ACP. We were in the backseat and absolutely shocked by the turn of events. And by the time I had somewhat recovered from the shock, one of the men had smashed the window next to me, unlocked the car and placed a gun on my forehead. One of the other men then took away all our phones and wallets. I'm told the police haven't been able to find those yet.'

Manav's breathing was laboured. Agni realized that Manav, in his mind, was dangerously close to the moments in which the most traumatic events of that night had unfolded. Agni did not want to push him further down that path.

He stood up and thanked Manav profusely for his time.

When he was close to the door of the executive suite, Agni stopped and turned around, as if he had remembered something.

'Mr Chauhan, those three men have to say that this was a job they had been paid for. If they are right, then what they did inside Tipple was meant to provoke you to get into that brawl in front of dozens of eyewitnesses. It was premeditated. It was someone's idea to make the whole incident look like those three men retaliated for what had happened inside the club. Now, being one of the most successful entrepreneurs in the city, I'm sure you've more enemies than friends. Do you have anyone particular in mind?'

Manav almost gaped.

'That possibility never crossed my mind! As for my enemies, well, there are too many! Far too many of them.' He closed his eyes and almost whispered to his unknown adversary, 'But why drag Hiya into all this?'

There was an awkward silence inside the room for a few seconds, and then Agni said, 'Mr Chauhan, I know it will be difficult for you. But I will need to know more about the events of the last few months the next time we meet.'

Manav nodded, still staring at the slowly descending pall of darkness outside the glass windows.

Chapter 7

Three months back

Manav Chauhan, looking dapper in his pin-striped suit, natty tie and navy-blue shirt, left his chair and smiled warmly as Priyanka, his secretary, led the lady into his office.

'Good morning, Mr Chauhan. I'm Shilpa from *Business Today*. Thanks for your time this morning.' The journalist introduced herself, stretching out a rather cold hand.

Manav shook her hand. 'Have a seat, please. What would you like to have? Everyone loves the filter coffee in my office.'

The charm that Manav Chauhan exuded was overpowering. Shilpa looked overwhelmed. She managed a feeble nod, setting in place over an ear a few unruly strands of her hair.

Manav turned towards Priyanka who had been waiting for Shilpa to make up her mind about her choice of beverage. Manav made the decision for Shilpa, to the latter's relief.

'Would you send in two cups of filter coffee for us, please, Priyanka? Thanks.' He smiled. 'And no calls for the next one hour please.'

Turning back to the journalist, he said, 'Shilpa, I'm really sorry I've had to cancel this interview thrice over the last two weeks. I've been travelling almost every day, and everything seems to... '

Manav's phone buzzed.

He looked at the screen and rejected the call with a swipe of his thumb.

Shilpa, in the meantime, had placed the recorder on the table and was getting ready to start the interview. She had been eyeing this assignment for months now. Manav, on the other hand, looked forward to the interview himself. It was every entrepreneur's dream to appear on the cover of Business Today.

'Mr Chauhan, I completely understand. And I have to say this—you've been really nice. Not everyone offers an alternate slot every time we miss one.'

The coffee arrived, interrupting the conversation briefly.

Once the cups with the steaming coffee and the plates with cookies had been laid out, Shilpa was on her mark.

'Shall we start, Mr Chauhan?'

'Whenever you are ready,' Manav smiled, taking a sip of the coffee. He reclined on his chair, his eyes fixed on Shilpa.

'Tell me, what made you get into this business? Were you driven by your passion, or, is this something you were destined to do, inheriting the business from your illustrious father?'

'I have always been asked that question. It is true that I inherited a real estate business from my father, and a very successful one at that. However, you must agree, I changed the face of that business and the face of this city in the process. The shopping malls I built are comparable to the best in the world and more and more global brands are queuing up for space in our properties.'

'A number of trade *pundits* have criticised your decision of investing heavily in Kolkata.'

'I don't agree. When I look at Kolkata today, I see a city in the cusp of change. The purchasing power of the upper middle class...'

Manav's phone buzzed again. He looked at the screen and rejected the call, again.

He took a sip of the coffee and was about to speak when the phone buzzed, yet again.

This time, he looked apologetically at Shilpa and said, 'Can I take this, if you don't mind?'

'Sure, Mr Chauhan. Please go ahead.'

Manav walked across the room to an antechamber, closing the door behind him.

'How many times do I have to tell you not to call me when I'm at work?' Manav held the phone close to his mouth as he spoke into it. 'Unless someone's dying! And why don't you get it? I rejected your call twice. Isn't that a more than subtle message that I'm busy?' Manav paced up and down the small room. 'There's a journalist from Business Today in my room and I am in the middle of an interview.'

'But Manav, baby, we're getting late for our lunch date.'

'I repeat, I'm in the middle of an interview, Neha, for god's sake! And we never planned for a lunch date today.' Manav was livid, almost shouting into the phone now. He was sure there was no lunch date with Neha in his calendar that afternoon.

'What? Now your fiancée has to make an appointment with you for lunch? I feel like being with you for lunch, and that's it! I'm coming down to your office to pick you up—*now*. Just say goodbye to that boring journo. Or, let me guess, is she hot?'

Manav could hear giggles in the background. So, Neha was with her stupid friends. He was probably on speaker, and Neha was trying to show off her absolute control over her fiancé's schedule.

'Neha, I don't have time for this nonsense!'

'Baby, we also planned to go for lingerie shopping for the wedding, remember?' Neha tried to sound sexy, her voice suddenly turning husky with renewed giggles in the background.

'Fuck the lingerie and fuck the wedding!' Manav screamed into the phone and ended the call. He clutched the phone tight in his fist and clenched his teeth, banging his forehead on the wooden panel on the wall.

After a while, Manav walked out of the antechamber, looking distraught, his face flushed.

Shilpa had heard him and stood up, spilling coffee on her skirt in the process. She was desperately looking for a tissue. The recorder had been turned off a while back.

'I... I am sorry, Shilpa. Can we do this some other time?' Manav did not look at her, visibly embarrassed, as he headed towards the door. 'Priyanka, please apologise to the lady on my behalf and escort her out,' Shilpa heard him say as he walked out of his cabin, closing the door behind him.

Chapter 8

Manav emptied the glass of whiskey and looked down from his balcony at the sparse late-night traffic on the road below, the monsoon breeze ruffling his hair. There was a light drizzle.

He let out a deep sigh. It was clearly not working.

The Awasthis and the Chauhans had been close for three generations. Deepak Awasthi, Neha's father, and Surinder Chauhan, Manav's father, were successful entrepreneurs with impeccable acumen, whose respective businesses in restaurants and real estate had flourished even when the climate in the state had not been too favourable for running a successful business. The two families came together in a number of business ventures, and that only helped to strengthen the bond between them. When the two families decided to get Manav and Neha married, Neha was happy while Manav was not too sure.

With the wedding now less than a month away, Manav was finding it increasingly difficult to handle Neha with every passing day. It was the third time they had fought bitterly in the last two weeks.

The last time, Manav had walked out of a restaurant in the middle of what was supposed to be a romantic dinner with his fiancée. On that occasion, Neha went on and on about what she considered was Manav's 'waning interest' in their relationship. She was certain that Manav did not find her attractive anymore, as Manav had spurned her sexual advances on a few occasions.

That girl was bringing out the worst in him and Manav could not let that continue.

He fumbled in his pockets, looking for his phone. He had to call Neha.

'Is she asleep?' Manav pondered for a second.

It did not matter, he decided.

He had had enough. He did not want to lose a good friend, trying to make her a wife.

Chapter 9

Manav looked around the room at the grim faces of the elders.

He had barely got out of bed that morning when he was summoned to the living room, downstairs. When he made the phone call the previous night, he had no idea that the entire Awasthi clan would flock to his house at daybreak. Neha was not making eye contact. Her eyes were swollen. She must have cried all night.

'Manav, it's perfectly understandable if the two of you have had a tiff. You are young and wedding preparations can be stressful. You have a business to run, and my daughter can be very unreasonable at times...' Deepak Awasthi started off in a conciliatory tone. The effort showed.

Manav spoke after a while.

'This is not a lovers' tiff. This is not working, Uncle. I have thought this through.'

'And when did you find the time to *think* this through?' Surinder Chauhan roared. 'Last night? Over your whiskey?'

'Manav, the two of you have known each other for many years...' Deepak Awasthi continued. Manav did not let him finish.

'Yes, Uncle. But I don't think that means we should get married!'

Deepak Awasthi looked miffed. The mask of sobriety had finally slipped.

'And you realize this *now*? With less than a month to go before the wedding?'

He cast a sympathetic glance towards his daughter. He then looked at Manav's parents with mute pleas of decidedly dismissing what he thought were mere whims of a wealthy bachelor, and then, he glared back at Manav.

Surinder Chauhan looked into Manav's eyes and asked, 'You've met someone else, haven't you? Probably during one of your business tours, or, in the office...'

Manav raised a hand.

'Let's not make things nasty here, Dad.'

'You think *I'm* making things nasty? You didn't bother to think twice about Neha! You didn't bother to think about us! In case you don't realize, let me remind you that you are playing with people's feelings here!'

Surinder Chauhan started pacing the room swiftly, his hands clasped tightly behind him.

Deepak Awasthi sat facing Manav, his eyes fixed on him. He eventually lost patience and yelled, 'Look at you... sitting there like a picture of serenity when all of us are so upset, so agitated by your idiotic decision! Is this how your parents raised you?'

'Enough!' Manav finally lost his composure at the mention of his upbringing. He shot up from his chair and headed towards his room.

'Well, this is it, I guess! Looks like there isn't anything left to discuss here.' Deepak Awasthi stood up. The colour had risen on his chubby face, there were sweat patches on his shirt. His wife and daughter followed his cue.

The mothers exchanged furtive glances. Surinder Chauhan cast a reproachful glance towards his son and then took a step towards his childhood friend, Deepak Awasthi. The latter's hands, however, were firmly ensconced inside his trousers' pockets.

As the Awasthis marched out of the living room, Neha stopped in her tracks and turned towards the receding frame of Manav.

'Manav, it was stupid of me to believe we'd be together for a lifetime!' said Neha as she threw the engagement ring at Manav. 'Looks like you have other plans.'

Manav stopped and turned towards Neha. He said, 'Neha, we can still be friends. That's exactly what I want too. This marriage thing...'

Neha did not let Manav finish. As her tears spilled over, there was suddenly an uncharacteristic, almost menacing, steely resolve in Neha's tone. 'I know you'll come back to me, Manav. I'll make sure you do! *You* will put that ring back on my finger.'

Deepak Awasthi put an arm around his daughter's shoulder and said, 'I swear by the tears you have shed in this house, I will get to the bottom of this!'

***

Later that evening, Deepak Awasthi was in the balcony adjacent to his bedroom with a glass of his favourite single malt. His dishevelled hair ruffled by the breeze and his vision blurred by the whiskey, he let out a deep sigh and looked up at the stars and a pale white sliver of moon on the ink-black sky.

China Valley was one of the oldest restaurants in South Kolkata. It started off back in the seventies. It was the brainchild of Prahlad Awasthi, Deepak Awasthi's father. Prahlad Awasthi was a visionary. Within a few years of its inception, the restaurant became the talk of the town.

China Valley kept growing through the eighties and nineties, launching new properties and takeaway counters in different parts of Kolkata. Around 2005, Deepak even planned expansion beyond Kolkata. And then, a few years back, the slump kicked in.

The city suddenly had several new options. Global chains started making inroads. People started experimenting with different kinds of cuisines. Kolkata became more cosmopolitan, which had an influence on the city's culinary habits. Shopping malls started flourishing. Dining got linked with a day out in the mall or a movie in a multiplex inside the same mall. That did not augur well for several traditional, stand-alone restaurants. China Valley was no exception.

China Valley, and Deepak Awasthi, had been struggling ever since to keep up, having lost the patronage of a large section of the elite. Deepak had recently had to pull the shutters down on a few outlets in North Kolkata. Business down south was not looking good either.

With Manav calling the wedding off, Deepak's plans were shattered even before they had had a chance to take off.

His thoughts were interrupted as his wife Mansi walked into the balcony.

'Enough, Deepak! You've been drinking since sundown. Get something to eat now,' Mansi said.

'I'm not hungry,' Deepak replied without looking at her, 'why don't you have dinner and go to bed?' Deepak sounded eager to get rid of her.

Mansi walked up to her husband and stood next to him. Stroking his back, she said, 'Deepak, I know you are hurt. And so is our daughter. She hasn't had anything to eat since the time we came back from the Chauhans' house. But, as her parents, we should not lose hope and give up. We must stay strong and stand by our daughter. She needs you next to her in this hour of crisis.' She paused briefly and said, 'So what if Manav doesn't want to marry our daughter? She is pretty, runs a business of her own, and most importantly, she is an Awasthi, the family that owns China Valley! We will have a long queue of suitors in front of our house. I don't see why we should slip into despair!'

'Because the Awasthis are finished! China fucking Valley is finished!' Deepak turned around and screamed so loudly that Mansi stepped a few inches back. The whiskey spilled on his shirt. Deepak grabbed his wife by her arms and said, 'Why don't you get it? Manav was my last and only chance!'

'What... what do you mean?' Mansi could barely speak, yet to recover from the shock of the sudden revelation.

Deepak sat down on a chair and poured more whiskey into his glass. He took a generous swig and put the glass down. He sat with his eyes closed and ran his fingers through his hair. After a few minutes, he blew out from his mouth and when he spoke again, he sounded more composed.

'I had a plan to revive the business. China Valley could benefit if we started operating from outlets inside some of the shopping malls in town. The footfall is high, especially with families trooping in during the weekends. We could target some of the best-paid people in town with propensity to spend.'

Mansi, who had started picking up the ropes of the business, reflected on Deepak's plan for a few minutes and said, 'You can never be sure. There would be stiff competition from some of the global chains that already have outlets in the malls. Not to mention the high rents these restaurants end up paying. I heard the restaurants have to pay either a flat rental or part with a percentage of their revenue, whichever the mall authorities find juicier.'

'You are right, Mansi,' Deepak bent forward, his eyes shining in the dark, 'And that's where it helps to have the mall owner in the family, as your *daamaad* to be precise. You get room for negotiations, you see.' Deepak emptied his glass. He sighed and said, 'But Manav's decision changes everything!'

Deepak reclined on his chair and closed his eyes, perfectly motionless. The only sound in the balcony was that of the wind rustling through the leaves of the trees in the lawn. Mansi opened her mouth to coax her husband into having dinner but decided against it. She realized that Deepak needed the time to come to terms with the developments earlier in the day, which she now knew had changed the course of not just their daughter's life, but that of the family business too. Her experience from the years she had spent with Deepak told her that she could make her daughter see sense and move on, but not the man next to her.

Mansi wondered if Deepak had fallen asleep. She was proved wrong the very next moment as Deepak suddenly sprang up from the chair. He looked around for his phone. It was on the low table in front of Mansi. She picked it up and handed it over to Deepak.

'Who do you want to call so late?' she asked, her voice trembling. There was something not quite right about her husband's demeanour, and he was drunk beyond his wits.

'I will not let Manav Chauhan get away with this! If there is another girl warming his bed, I will find her out and finish her!' Deepak almost hissed.

Mansi's heart skipped a beat. She knew that her husband could go to any length when it came to matters related to the business. She had seen him walk on the wrong side of the law and get away on many occasions in the past. The man had friends in all the right places.

'Who are you calling?' Mansi repeated her question.

'Lakhan, Manav's chauffeur,' Deepak replied with a crooked smile even as he scrolled for the number, 'if the boss is hanging around with another girl, the chauffeur will know!'

***

The next Saturday evening, Manav was at the opening of Prestige Mall. The who's who of the city had turned up for the inauguration of the plush new property of the Chauhans. The police had a tough time managing the hordes of men and women who had been filling up the adjoining roads since the afternoon, the light drizzle notwithstanding.

One of the guests of honour for the event that evening was the heartthrob of the city—actress Hiya Sen.

Chapter 10

Hiya lost her parents in a train accident when she was seven and was brought up by an uncle who worked in the local post office in a small town in Burdwan. Her aunt stitched dresses and made candles when she found time from cooking in a working women's hostel, travelling by train to Kolkata and back every day. Everything that had been worth anything in the household had already been sold. There was just about enough to eat, the roof leaked in the monsoons in certain parts of the house and the windows made creaking sounds on stormy nights.

However, Hiya's life in that run-down house next to the railway tracks away from the din and the shine of the city had a purpose which made every tomorrow worth waiting for.

The local club would often organize late night movie shows in one of the fields in the neighbourhood. A decrepit projector would beam on a crumpled piece of cloth, with gaping holes here and there, movies with stories of larger-than-life heroes and heroines whose rags-to-riches journeys filled Hiya's young eyes with dreams. She wanted to be one of them.

Hiya lived in a world of her own. She talked to herself when she was alone and fell back on her own instincts when she had to make choices. When she was in the third year of her Arts course in college, she filled out the application form for a beauty pageant in Kolkata, much against the wishes of her uncle. She gave up her studies and headed for the city. She won the crown. Modelling assignments, photoshoots for popular magazines, roles in television serials, and then movies—everything happened in quick succession and Hiya never had the time to stop and think. Opportunities kept knocking on her door, and her talent propelled her to dizzying heights of fame in an incredibly short time.

With fame, came money. And the men—much-married senior actors, wealthy heads of production houses, lecherous politicians and businessmen she ran into at social gatherings. But, Hiya was not to be won over with money and favours. She wanted to feel unbridled love in her heart for someone, rather than be pampered by expensive gifts from her admirers. She missed having someone in her life whom she would feel like cuddling with after a long day, on the couch in front of the TV with a tub of popcorn, or someone she would just be happy buying things for even if he did not need any of those. She missed being unreasonably possessive about someone. She wanted every romantic song she heard or acted in to throw up images of her in the arms of that special someone. She wanted someone to think of when it rained, and the earth smelt sweet. She waited for a name she could whisper with her heart and soul, while clinging to her pillows under a warm blanket on a cold winter night. She spent her days and nights with that dream. And when she would meet him, there would be chimes in the air and a light drizzle, and an unruly breeze would play with her *dupatta* before his passionate gaze— like a scene from one of her movies.

And then she met Manav at the inauguration of one of his shopping malls. Love caught her unawares as her eyes locked with his, refusing to be blinded for once by the dazzle of flashbulbs.

For the first time in many years, she did not see lust in a man's eyes.

Chapter 11

Present Day

As Agni and Arya drove across the bridge over the railway tracks, Agni could not help but smile at the glorious co-existence of opposites that made his city so special.

He could see the teeming crowds on the platform at the station, the run-down shanties on both sides of the railway tracks, scantily clad kids playing around and women going about their daily chores nonchalantly as trains sped by their shacks. Their ears were used to the relentless drumming of the trains on the tracks, and Agni wondered if they would be able to sleep at all, if they were put up in more serene surroundings.

Overlooking the station and the measly existence of the slum dwellers were flats for the middle-class that had seen better days. The walls had been stripped of colours and some of the windows had only a hinge to hold on to. Agni looked at the potted plants and the clotheslines that decorated the balconies. He saw men reclining on their chairs with their cups of morning tea and newspapers, the women freshly bathed hanging out clothes to dry, and children getting ready for school. He felt the flats, however run down, had an aura of middle-class security and offered its dwellers a feeling of comfort, even in hardship, which they had probably gotten used to over the years. It was, again, rather unlikely that their occupants would choose to migrate to a more congenial but unfamiliar environment, even if such an opportunity ever presented itself.

Driving through the squalor, they crossed Kasba and just as the backdrop in a stage play changes between consecutive acts, they found themselves surrounded by plush apartment complexes, office spaces, retail outlets of global brands, and a sprawling new shopping mall, with a movie multiplex.

It was this mall that was their destination that morning.

To be more specific, they were headed towards a boutique inside that mall, by the name of Panache, which was owned by Neha Awasthi.

As they stepped into the boutique, they were greeted by a soft warm fragrance of lavender wafting around the shop. Agni's eyes went to dresses of esoteric design that connoisseurs of fashion would not hesitate to spend their fortunes on. His eyes went to a picture of Manav Chauhan inaugurating the boutique with a bunch of happy women around him.

A girl walked up to Agni and Arya with curiosity writ large upon her face. The two policemen obviously did not look anything like the usual customers which the boutique attracted.

'I am ACP Agni Mitra and this is my colleague Inspector Arya Sen. We would like to meet Ms Neha Awasthi,' Agni said.

'Ma'am has stepped out for a bit. She'll be back anytime.'

'May we?' Agni gestured towards a sofa set.

The girl was visibly alert. 'Umm... yes, sure. Please do have a seat,' she said, 'I'm Anamika. I manage the store during the day.'

Agni looked around the store. Pointing towards the woman standing next to Manav in the picture, he asked, 'Is that Ms Awasthi?'

'Oh... I thought you knew her!' The surprise in her tone almost bordered on suspicion.

'I have heard about her, though we've never met. I doubt if she knows me.' Agni turned around to face her and smiled.

The girl sat opposite Agni.

'How long have you been working here, Anamika?' asked Agni.

'Almost a year now.'

'Right from the time Panache was launched?'

'Yes, sir.'

'That's Manav Chauhan, right?' Agni pointed to the picture.

'Yes, sir. He inaugurated our boutique.' Anamika smiled. 'Well, it's *his* mall!'

'Of course, it is!' Agni reclined on the sofa. 'Does he visit the store frequently?'

Anamika hesitated. Agni bent forward with his eyes fixed on her.

'Well... err, he used to. But he suddenly stopped coming here. I haven't seen him in the store for a while.'

'When was the last time you saw him here?'

Anamika tried to remember.

'Must be close to four months, sir.'

'I see. You do know that he is in a hospital right now, don't you?'

'Oh yes! The news was all over the internet!'

'You got to know from the internet! Wasn't the incident discussed in Panache?' Agni smiled.

Anamika kept looking at the floor. She looked up and was about to say something, but held back. She looked restless, unable to make up her mind.

The conversation was interrupted by the sound of heels clicking on the polished floor. Agni turned around to see a stunningly attractive woman walking in. Her hair was tied back in a ponytail and she wore large silver hoops. A fitted purple shirt and clingy black pants accentuated her curves.

Agni and Arya stood up as the woman approached them. Anamika stood nervously at attention.

After the introductions and exchange of pleasantries, Neha Awasthi sat down facing the two policemen.

'Gentlemen, I'm so sorry you had to wait. I had to get into an urgent meeting with one of my suppliers,' Neha apologised.

'I completely understand,' Agni smiled disarmingly. 'I can assure you this won't take long.'

'Thanks... it's a busy day!' Neha almost warned him.

'Ms Awasthi, I understand your family is very close to the Chauhans.'

'Yes, they are like extended family.' Saying this, Neha hesitated for a minute and added, 'Well, almost.'

'I believe Mr Surinder Chauhan and Mr Deepak Awasthi go back a long way. The families decided to turn the business alliance into a social relationship by getting their children married.'

Neha nodded in concurrence.

'But the engagement was called off a few weeks before the wedding,' Agni went on, not taking his eyes off Neha even for a second.

Neha looked up. Arya detected a fleeting glimpse of hurt in her eyes.

'Manav was not ready at that time,' she almost whispered.

'I see. How did you feel about that incident?'

Neha looked into Agni's eyes and asked, 'What has that got to do with your investigation?'

'It's important for me to understand the circumstances leading up to Hiya's murder.'

'Where do I come in? Or, my family, for that matter? She was done in by a bunch of ruffians!'

'Well, let's just say, I'm exploring other possibilities.'

'What do you mean?'

'The attack on Mr Chauhan and Ms Sen might not have been impulsive, as it's being made out to be.'

Agni noticed the colour fade on Neha's face.

'That's what makes it important for me to probe deeper into the events of the last few months.'

'Are you accusing me of...'

Agni did not let her finish. 'I'm not accusing you of anything. As I said, I'm only gathering information. I repeat my question. How did you feel about the wedding being called off by Mr Chauhan with less than a month to go?'

'I was shattered, of course. What else can you expect?' Neha paused briefly and continued, 'I had accepted Manav as the man I would spend the rest of my life with. I had started dreaming of a future with him and planning for it to minute details, just like any other girl. And then...' Agni could see tears welling up in Neha's eyes. She took time to regain her composure and then declared, 'I don't want to go back to those days.'

'You were hurt. Were you angry?' Agni did not pay heed to her pronouncement.

Neha looked up and locked her eyes with Agni. 'I don't know where you're going with this, ACP!'

'You didn't answer me, Ms Awasthi.'

'You know, ACP, the line between hurt and rage can be very thin.' There was a wry smile on Neha's face. The icy cold tone of her voice made Arya's heart skip a beat. Neha was almost challenging the two men to gauge her true feelings.

'Were you close to Ms Sen?'

Neha smiled again. 'You mean Hiya? Well... she was the darling of the masses. Manav had decided to marry a showgirl! How does it matter whether I was close to her or not?'

'That doesn't answer my question!'

'ACP, what do you expect? I'd be thick friends with a girl married to the man who ditched me almost at the altar?'

'That's a better answer,' Agni smiled. 'Have you been to the hospital to meet Manav?'

There was a sudden rush of cheer on Neha's face. Her eyes lit up as she said, 'We meet every day! I'm there usually in the evenings.'

'You look happy, Ms Awasthi.'

There was a swift change in Neha's demeanour. She looked alert.

'I've never had any hesitation to admit that I love Manav. And I won't hesitate to tell you this, ACP—I feel happy to be around him as he copes with his loss. To be of help, in whatever little way I can.'

'I can see that you've moved on. Do you regret having harboured your anger and negative feelings towards Ms Sen and perhaps, Mr Chauhan?'

Neha looked up. Her jaws were stiff.

'It was quite natural for me to feel that way, ACP. I have no regrets.' She looked at her watch and said, 'And now if you are done, I have a few calls to make.'

Agni and Arya stood up to leave.

***

As Agni and Arya were on their way out of the mall, Agni heard a woman call him by his name and he turned around. It was Anamika, the girl they had met inside Panache.

'Sir, we didn't get to finish our conversation...'

'Indeed!' Agni said, as Arya and he exchanged glances. 'Although, I didn't realize you had more to say.'

'Ma'am is usually not here in the evenings these days. I get relieved around six. If you can come back around five...'

Chapter 12

Agni was back in Panache around five that evening.

'It's about Ma'am...' Anamika started hesitatingly after the initial exchange of pleasantries had been done away with.

Agni sat up straight.

'What *about* her?' Agni was intrigued.

Anamika looked around her. Agni had not seen a single customer come into the store since he had walked in. That had been his observation during his morning visit as well, which did not make a favourable impression about the state of the business. Agni wondered for a split second how Neha managed the rental. The next moment, he reminded himself that the owner of the mall had been her fiancé once, and the two families were friends. That might have led to favourable commercial arrangements.

'Uh... um... It seems odd to me...' Anamika hesitated again, 'please don't quote me...'

'I won't,' Agni smiled reassuringly.

'You know... they were supposed to get married...' Anamika paused.

'You mean, Ms Awasthi and Mr Chauhan?' Agni checked.

'Yes.'

'So I heard,' Agni concurred.

'They were engaged. I saw the ring...' Anamika paused briefly. 'And then, something went wrong. Mr Chauhan married the heroine.'

Agni smelt a whiff of resentment at the way Anamika referred to Hiya by her profession, instead of using her name. Anamika, apparently, was not too happy about Manav calling off the wedding with her boss with less than a month to go.

'Ma'am was devastated. She would hide from us in one of the changing rooms and cry. I heard her...'

'I don't find anything odd in that! Don't you think that was quite natural?' Agni asked.

'You are right... nothing odd about that. Everyone was shocked. And then, she changed. She plunged into work. This boutique became her world. She didn't speak much. At times, she was very rude to everyone around her. The girl who stitches for us, and Pratik—he keeps accounts for us—no one was spared. Not even me! She yelled at me a couple of times. She later said that she had felt I had not been professional enough with some of the customers!'

Agni did not find that unusual. With the moving away of a loved one, something hardens inside. You embrace the rigours of the daily grind, amplified manifold, to escape the hurt. The world sees you as more efficient, more energetic than ever, but that is just the veneer behind which you are hiding your broken heart. You become more practical in a ruthless way, which sometimes makes you look a bit threatening to the world around.

Anamika continued, 'And then the mishap happened. I was home having my morning tea when I read the news. I thought about ma'am and I couldn't wait to see her. I wasn't even sure if she would *be* here in the boutique. But when I arrived, she was already here! Her father was with her too. Later, they left for the hospital where Manav sir had been admitted.' Anamika stopped.

'How did you find her coping with the news?' asked Agni.

The hesitation was back. 'Sir, I may be wrong. After all, it's just the way *I* looked at it. But ma'am looked like her usual self after months! It was as if... how do I say it? It seemed to me as if a dark shadow had finally slipped off her face...'

'How did Mr Awasthi behave?'

'When I came in, I saw him hugging ma'am. He told her to have faith in god. It seemed... umm... please don't quote me, sir... as if they were relieved! It didn't look like someone close to them had been brutally beaten up and lost his newly-married wife just hours back!'

'How has Ms Awasthi been ever since?'

'Absolutely fine, sir. She is very nice to us, like she used to be before that phase. She goes to the hospital every evening to visit Mr Chauhan, spending only the morning here. She looks happy. I have a feeling she believes they will get back together.'

'And what makes you say *that*?'

Anamika seemed to regret having made that comment. She cast another furtive glance towards the door.

'Sir, I should not be saying this... I will lose my job if ma'am gets to know...'

By then, Agni had realized that the girl was actually rather eager to share her story with anyone who cared to listen.

He gestured to her to continue.

'I overheard ma'am speaking to someone on the phone the other day. She said if she married anyone it would be Manav Chauhan and no one else. I wondered how she could be so confident...' Anamika paused for a moment and said, 'But then, come to think of it sir, Mr Chauhan is single again. And ma'am is taking good care of him...'

'I know what you mean.' Agni had wrinkles on his brow. Hiya's death had indeed turned out to be a trump card for Neha.

He looked at his watch and stood up. He thanked Anamika profusely, who pleaded with Agni one more time that, her opinion about her boss and more importantly, her eavesdropping should not be brought to Neha's attention.

Agni smiled and walked out of the store.

His phone buzzed.

It was Arya. He had spent the last few hours in Deepak Awasthi's office, making enquiries.

Chapter 13

'The business is in bad shape. They have closed a few outlets in North Kolkata. There are more closures on the cards,' Arya said as he sipped his coffee.

Agni's palms cradled his cup. His hands were cold. They were inside a Café Coffee Day outlet, close to the office of Awasthi Restaurants Pvt Ltd. in Gariahat.

Agni looked at the gang of boisterous college goers who circled a big round table, right opposite to theirs. 'I remember China Valley used to be a rage when I was in college in the nineties. Taking a girl to China Valley for dinner could win you brownie points and give you a head start among her suitors,' Agni smiled, taking a generous bite of the smoked chicken sandwich.

'Well... I could never afford a date in China Valley with my meagre pocket money,' Arya lamented, remembering his poor run of luck with his female classmates. 'Maybe that's why I never found favour with the girls!' he added regretfully.

Agni placed his hand on Arya's shoulder and said, 'I'm sure there were reasons beyond missed dinners at China Valley for your not getting lucky, my friend. Girls in colleges probably expect more than just good noodles from their male friends. But let's not digress.'

Arya brushed aside his adolescent regrets and continued, 'The restaurant chain has apparently lost out to competition from global brands opening eateries in the city, and also to changing tastes of the people.'

Agni used the paper napkin to wipe the mayonnaise off the edges of his lips, took a sip of his very strong black coffee and put down the mug.

'That means Deepak Awasthi's fortunes don't look good enough,' Agni said, throwing his head back and closing his eyes.

'Exactly,' Arya exclaimed, putting down his walnut brownie and brushing the crumbs off his trousers with the back of his hand.

The conversation suddenly stopped.

'What are you thinking?' Arya asked impatiently after a while.

Agni washed down the last bit of his sandwich with the coffee. After a few seconds, he said, 'I have a hypothesis. What if Deepak Awasthi was eyeing business benefits from his daughter's marriage to Manav? You may argue that the families have been close for many years and Deepak could have approached his friend for help anyway. But you see, being in a relationship can potentially open up opportunities and mutually beneficial arrangements more easily.'

Arya thumped the arm of his chair in excitement. 'Oh yes! Why didn't this occur to me?'

Agni continued, 'The daughter already has a boutique in one of Manav Chauhan's malls. The father was probably eyeing a bigger slice of the pie – a certain arrangement that would benefit his restaurants. Maybe for Deepak Awasthi, there was much more to that marriage than two childhood friends walking into the sunset holding hands.'

'If your hypothesis is right, then Manav Chauhan's sudden decision to call off his wedding with Neha must have put a spanner in the works!' Arya's excitement was palpable as he completed the chain of Agni's thoughts.

Agni finished off his coffee and continued, 'But don't forget that the Awasthis and the Chauhans are friends. A reconciliation is now possible. The daughter, in any case, has vowed to marry

Manav, come what may. That's what I heard from the girl working at her boutique and I have no reason to disbelieve her. Neha is already making up for lost time and lost opportunities, being with Manav as he copes with his loss. As for Manav, he may decide to move on, to try and get over the loss of his love and go back to Neha.'

'Wouldn't that be great news for Papa's wobbly restaurant business, among other benefits?'

'Exactly! Papa might have realized that, everyone would benefit from Hiya's death. All it would take is to hire some goons, stage an attack that leads to her death, and the circumstances would throw up a completely different motive without the actual beneficiaries coming under the scanner,' Agni said, rubbing his brow.

The two men left their seats.

'Manav Chauhan did mention that he has enemies. The question is how much we can trust his friends!' Arya exclaimed as they headed for the exit.

Agni was somewhat relieved to leave the café. The song they had been playing inside was from a Bollywood movie about a serial killer and it had been distracting Agni for the last several minutes, reminding him of the loss he had suffered a few years back when several women in Kolkata had fallen prey to a ruthless killer and the shadow of death had loomed large over the city.

Agni had nabbed the perpetrator, but not before Medha, his wife, had been killed.

Chapter 14

Agni pulled up the hood of his jacket and took a long swig of the whiskey, draining his glass. He was in the balcony of his flat, his eyes fixed on streetlights that looked dim through the light mist. With ornate decorations for the festive season all over, the South City Mall was a behemoth of concrete, steel and glass in the horizon. The illuminated interiors visible through the transparent walls looked depressingly desolate at this hour of the night.

A dog barked somewhere. A car swooshed by, its headlights forming cones in the mist. The only other sound came from the hammers of workers giving finishing touches to a pandal at a distance.

Agni put the empty glass down with a dull thud. He picked up his laptop and typed in the 'search' bar:

Tollywood actress Rituja

Rituja had been in his mind ever since he had seen her at the bar the other day.

His eyes went first to her pictures that charted her journey from the doe-eyed fresh-faced girl-next-door who had become the city's sweetheart overnight to the voluptuous sex symbol she had transformed into, inhibitions in front of the camera steadily slipping with every passing year in the recent past. In her interviews, she attributed that transformation to 'demands of roles' and 'changing tastes of the audience exposed to global cinema'. In reality, she had been struggling for a few years now to ward off competition from younger girls and much to the dismay of her fans, had resorted to cringeworthy exhibitionism to pull in the crowds, albeit with limited success.

Agni scrolled down the laptop screen, skimming through news reports about Rituja. As he neared the bottom of the page, he suddenly stopped. A report higher up had caught his eye.

He scrolled back up and opened a report that was headlined:

Tolly girls get into ugly spat

Agni read through the report:

Come to think about it. Movies are just like any other business, with people having conflicting opinions about each other, just as people working in an office would have. So, while you and I like to bitch about our colleagues, actors are no different!

However, what makes them special is the fact that while most of our snide remarks stay within our groups of friends in the canteen, the statements our celebrities make about each other kick off serious controversies and become headlines in dailies.

Yesterday, a sedate Tollywood studio was livened up by a spat between the seasoned diva Rituja Bose and reigning heartthrob Hiya Sen, who are working together in Aniruddha Goswami's under production movie.

Aniruddha Goswami, recipient of two National Awards, is making a foray into mainstream Bengali movies with his latest project, which is being viewed as possibly the best, and the last opportunity for Rituja Bose to rise from the ashes and make a comeback after a string of flops.

The two heroines make no effort to hide their now famous animosity on the sets. Rituja Bose, without any doubt, is not among the admirers of Hiya Sen, considering the latter's meteoric rise in the industry and the number of projects with large production houses, which Rituja has reportedly lost to her younger co-star in the last couple of years.

Apparently, Rituja had been kept waiting for hours for a scene she was to shoot with Hiya, who turned up characteristically late. Rituja walked up to her and making sure that she was heard by all and sundry, including a number of journalists, said, "So you finally found the time from f***ing your millionaire friends!" Rituja, of course, had been referring to Hiya's rich and famous friends, especially the dishy Manav Chauhan, whom she is reportedly dating.

Not one to take the public humiliation lying down, Hiya retorted, again within earshot of everyone around, "I don't take this to my heart, you know. You're a f***ing fossil who's probably not getting any. I understand your frustration!"

Rituja walked out of the sets immediately.

If rumours are to be believed, Aniruddha Goswami, on Hiya's insistence, is considering a replacement for Rituja further to this incident. This would undoubtedly spell doom for Rituja's already floundering career.

Knowing Rituja Bose over the years as a woman who can go to any length to settle scores with her enemies, we wait with bated breath for the aftermath of this shockingly public fallout.

Agni looked up from the laptop screen, his mind drifting to another time in another world. Rituja Bose could indeed go to any length to have her way. No one knew it better than Agni. Images flashed before his eyes, images he had been trying to keep at bay all these years, images that reminded him of what could have turned out to be an early professional disaster. Seeing Rituja in person at the bar the other day had only prodded a wound that refused to heal with time.

A clock struck two somewhere at a distance, bringing Agni back to the present.

He looked at the date of the incident in the studio. It was a week before Hiya's wedding, nineteen days before her gruesome murder.

Chapter 15

Ten years back

'I'm told you are among the best we have and the right man for this job,' Deputy Commissioner Upadhyay looked at Agni and then around the room seeking corroboration. The other senior officials in the room nodded in affirmation.

Inspector Agni Mitra found it difficult to contain his elation that bubbled inside, but all that he said was 'Thank you, sir', with a deadpan face.

'As you have been briefed by ACP Bardhan, Rituja Bose, the famous actress, is being threatened by a stalker,' the Deputy Commissioner gestured to Agni to pull up a chair. 'It started with e-mails and phone calls at odd hours. Rituja tried to ward him off, first through polite dissuasion, and then by choosing to completely ignore his advances. Last week, someone sneaked into the backyard and broke into her house. Luckily, she was out on a shoot. That's when she realized she had had enough and decided to seek our help.

'We will need to offer protection and find the stalker. To start with, two armed constables will be positioned at her house round the clock. We will set up surveillance in the premises. We will also need to beef up her security when she appears in public events. And we want you, Agni, to oversee all the arrangements to her satisfaction, and bring the stalker to book. Do you have any question?'

'Do we have any idea who this person might be?' Agni asked.

'We have no idea at the moment. It seems the stalker is someone who's intent on causing harm—to her and to her property.'

'Could be one of her many admirers,' suggested ACP Bardhan with a smirk.

'I won't be surprised,' said the DCP.

'Did Rituja recognize the voice on the phone?' Agni asked.

'The man has never spoken to her. Rituja said she had only heard someone breathing heavy at the other end of the line every time. The calls are being made from public phone booths—a different one every time,' the DCP replied.

'Have we tracked the e-mails?' Agni asked again.

'Yes, Agni. No luck there as well. They were sent from nondescript neighbourhood cyber cafés, again a different one every time. As you know, these cafés never run proper identity checks of their customers.' The DCP sounded frustrated.

'Finally, how do we know it's a man?' Agni asked.

The DCP smiled. 'That's an interesting question. We came to that conclusion from the tone of the e-mails. Moreover, Rituja's security guards reported that they had seen a hooded man hanging around in the neighbourhood late in the night a couple of days before the break-in. The man reportedly had his eyes on Rituja's duplex bungalow. The guards assumed that he was a fan – one of the many who hover around her house round the clock, hoping to catch a glimpse. The guards didn't act at that time.'

'The man whom the guards saw might have been just that after all... a harmless fan,' Agni smiled back at the DCP.

'I don't deny. Though the security guards now feel that the same man could have been the intruder.'

'I'm assuming we have a description of this man,' Agni checked.

'We don't, unfortunately. The descriptions from the guards were inconsistent and weren't too helpful.' The DCP confirmed. 'Agni, I want you to get into action immediately.' He paused briefly and then said, 'You know, Rituja has connections in all the right places.' He smiled meaningfully.

Agni did not have any doubt. Rituja had of late been seen attending political rallies and events organised by the ruling party. He, of course, nursed a not-so-secret admiration for the actress, making it a point to watch each one of her movies, her political preferences notwithstanding.

Agni felt excited. Not just because he would have an opportunity to work in close quarters with Rituja, but also because his being put in charge of her security meant that there was growing confidence in his abilities among his superiors.

Chapter 16

Rituja walked into the ground floor hall with her secretary.

Agni stood in front of the glass door leading to the backyard, which the stalker had broken to get into her house a few days ago. It had been repaired recently.

He had come down to Rituja's house that morning to check the surveillance system that had been installed. He also wanted to check the ground floor hall where the stalker had broken into. He gave appropriate instructions to the armed constables who had been posted in the premises and to the ones who would accompany Rituja's security staff when she went out. Agni also wanted to have a word with Rituja herself to find out who she thought the stalker might be.

Agni turned towards the actress and his heart skipped several beats.

Rituja was in a lemon green top, and her jeans were a second skin. The aroma of musk wafted in the air. The heartthrob of millions stood at an arm's length from Agni. For a few seconds, Agni's favourite scenes from Rituja's movies unfurled themselves before his eyes like a showreel and words failed him. And then, he reminded himself of the business that had brought him there that morning.

Rituja pushed her shades up past her forehead. Her kohl-rimmed eyes landed on Agni, and stayed there for more than a few seconds.

'My, my...! Here's a good-looking cop!' Rituja exclaimed with surprising candour.

It was one thing to be confident about your looks and something quite different to be appraised from head to toe by the most desirable woman in town. Agni suddenly felt bare and vulnerable before his favourite actress. He was instantly conscious of the fact that he had missed his morning workout sessions all through the week, thanks to his erratic hours at work.

'ACP Bardhan did call me in the morning and said great things about you.' She looked into Agni's eyes and held the gaze. 'You do look the part for sure!' Rituja inched closer. 'I can breathe easy now. I'm in safe hands.'

However gratifying her compliments might have been, Agni thought he should remind her that he was not her bodyguard— definitely not her Kevin Costner fantasy. But he held himself back, and said instead, 'Ms Bose, I wanted to talk to you about this stalker. If you have some time now, we can...'

Rituja did not let him finish. 'Listen,' Rituja said, 'I'll have to leave now for a shoot. Are you going to come along with me? We can talk on the way.' She almost sounded like a helpless child afraid to go out in the dark.

'There are a couple of armed constables who will accompany you, Ms Bose,' Agni smiled reassuringly. 'Don't worry. You'll be fine. I'll come back later. When will you be back?'

'I will be back in the afternoon,' Rituja said. She then came a few inches closer and said, 'Call me Ritu, please.' She smiled warmly, running her fingers through her curls.

Before Agni could respond, she turned around and walked out of the room.

Agni was still in a trance.

Chapter 17

Present day

Agni drove past St. Paul's Cathedral, that fascinating specimen of Indo-Gothic architecture, standing tall in its serene and tranquil gardens right in the middle of the racket of the city, the bright morning sun reflecting from its steeple.

As he passed by Victoria Memorial, Agni noticed holidaying crowds make a beeline for the decked-up horse carriages for a ride by the *maidan* and the Fort William grounds.

Agni had started early, and the autumn mist still hung over the vast expanse of the maidan, the skyscrapers beyond the greens forming smoky outlines on the clear blue sky. The traffic was yet to peak, and it was only the odd horse carriage chugging along leisurely that slowed Agni down.

He was headed for a shooting location not far away. He had set up an appointment with Rituja Bose through her secretary.

The shooting lasted for a couple more hours after Agni had arrived at the spot. He walked around in the gardens, teeming with holiday crowds and curious bystanders, and frequently checked his watch. From time to time, he checked on the progress of the shoot, its slow pace beginning to get on his nerves. He could see the director and the cinematographer, both of whom seemed to be quite agitated for reasons not immediately apparent to Agni. The centre of attention, of course, was Rituja who was in a skimpy knee-length yellow dress, romancing her hero, whom

Agni did not recognize. He looked several years younger than Rituja. The song being picturised played on loop, as the pair, with their non-existent chemistry, and the dancers in the background tried to get their moves right.

When the director was finally satisfied, Rituja walked up to her vanity van. Her secretary whispered something into her ears, pointing at Agni who stood a few feet away.

'Of course, I know him,' Rituja dismissed her secretary with a sweep of her hand and turned to face Agni. 'Come in,' she said, her eyes locked with his.

Agni followed her into her vanity van.

Agni had always felt that Rituja looked better without her loud make-up. the kind that she had on now. Her hair was done for the shoot, her black eyes hypnotic as always. She sat with her legs crossed, the short dress riding high on her ample thighs.

She lit a Marlboro Light and looked at Agni. 'You don't mind, I hope. I remember you didn't mind, when we last met.' She did not allow Agni to speak. 'How long has it been, Agni?' She asked, blowing the smoke off the corner of her mouth.

'Ten years...' Agni paused and then added, 'and four months.'

'You've been counting! That's so sweet! Long time, huh?'

'Long time, indeed.'

'I keep reading about you. You are doing well for yourself!' She blew out again and gazed at Agni with cold appraising eyes. Agni wished he could figure out what was going on in her mind, but her blinding beauty got in the way, like a veil through which it was difficult to see her true self.

'Ms Bose...'

Rituja stopped him.

'Call me Ritu, please.'

Agni went on, 'If you don't mind, I wanted to talk to you about Hiya Sen.'

'Ah, poor girl!' Rituja took a long drag and looked at Agni with narrowed eyes. 'Are *you* in charge of the case now? I thought I saw a different name in the papers.'

'I'm trying to do my bit.'

'Of course. I'd love to help. The whole thing was so shocking! It was unbelievable! We were shooting together for Aniruddha's movie just a few days before it happened...' her voice drifted away. She kept smoking silently for a few seconds, her eyes fixed on the floor. She then looked back at Agni and asked, 'What do you want to know?'

'You said that the two of you were working together at that time...'

'We were! And then she went away for her big, fat wedding.' The sarcasm in her tone was not lost on Agni.

'There were reports of friction on the sets between the two of you.' Agni did not want to waste time beating about the bush.

Rituja suddenly burst out laughing. 'So, the super cop also finds time for gossip mags?' She stamped over the cigarette butt and lit another.

She smoked silently again for a few seconds and then said, 'Well, let's just say we had our differences.'

'I believe the two of you had a bitter exchange of words on the sets of Aniruddha Goswami's film. I also heard that the project was very important for you.' Agni chose his words carefully.

'Every project is important for me, Agni. I'm not sure where you're going with these questions.' Her eyes narrowed again.

'I read she had insulted you in front of the press. There was also a suggestion in the report that, further to the altercation, the director realized that the two of you could not be allowed to continue to work together, as the conflict was slowing down the shoot. He had to let one of you go. And he considered replacing *you* with another senior actress,' Agni paused and added, 'and you aren't the forgiving sort, are you?'

Their eyes met for a split second, during which Agni's own words raked up tormenting memories. Agni wondered if Rituja's mind too had raced back a decade during that fraction of a second. Even if it did, Rituja had the acting chops to not let it show.

'Agni, let's stop beating about the bush,' Rituja sounded impatient. 'Are you, for reasons best known to you, suggesting that I had a role to play in Hiya's murder? That's absolutely ridiculous, as the whole world knows that she was raped and killed by a group of hooligans, for god's sake!'

'You didn't answer me.'

'Look, I've been in the industry for more than twelve years now. I worship my work. I find it difficult to get along with girls who take this up as just another glamorous job! A job that'll eventually get them loads of money and a rich husband.'

'Is that how you thought Hiya was?' Agni further asked.

'Do I *have* to say this? And what difference does it make? I mean, she's dead now!'

'It won't hurt. You're only helping me get to know her better.'

'Alright! If I *have* to tell you, I didn't rate her too high on discipline,' Rituja lit her third cigarette and added, 'and morals. Maybe because her rise was fast. She got everything served on a silver platter, without having to work too hard.'

'Why do you say that?'

'What would you say about a girl who first gets engaged to a millionaire who has but recently broken off his wedding, then has a fling on the side with a model which almost leads to a breakup with the rich bloke, and finally decides to dump the poor guy to go back to her millionaire fiancé and get married? In the meantime, her work suffers while she has all the fun.' Rituja looked agitated. She took a few quick drags and continued, 'Hiya kept cancelling shoots. The producers ran up huge losses. She would keep senior actors waiting for hours without showing any respect. And never felt sorry for her actions!' Rituja stopped, trying hard to get a hold on her anger. Her cheeks were flushed.

Agni was watching and listening for any sign that Rituja was lying or exaggerating, but her words came out easily, and with surprising honesty.

'Did you mention a *fling on the side* while she was engaged to Manav Chauhan?' stressed Agni.

'Everyone knew about it. She had a torrid affair with Mayank Kapoor.' Rituja shook her head, trying to get a strand of hair off her face, and reached for a can of Diet Coke.

'You mean the guy who models for the Chauhans' malls and housing complexes? I read in a tabloid the other day that he also acts in TV serials these days.' Agni refused the soft drink Rituja offered him with a gesture of his hand.

'Yes... he's the one! Mayank was shattered. He's doing a movie now, by the way. I'm helping him gather the pieces of his life.'

Rituja finished her smoke.

There was a knock on the door of her van.

'Ma'am, we are ready,' informed the assistant.

Rituja stood up. She looked into Agni's eyes.

'What are your plans this Friday?' Agni did not miss the flirtatious tone of Rituja's voice.

Agni's heart skipped a beat. Memories came flooding back.

'Do you want to meet Mayank? You could come with me on Friday night,' Rituja winked and asked, 'What were you thinking?'

Chapter 18

◇◇◇◇◇◇◇◇◇◇◇

Ten years back

Agni was ushered in by one of Rituja's female attendants as he walked in through the main door that opened into the spacious ground floor hall.

'Ma'am is upstairs. She has returned from the shoot a while back,' said the girl as she escorted Agni up the staircase.

The staircase ended in a lounge with a plush settee and a few chairs tossed around. There was a low table at the centre of the room. Agni could see a bottle of Glenlivet, an unfinished glass and an ash tray brimming with cigarette stubs. A door at the other end of the lounge, facing the settee, led to a bedroom.

The temperature inside was too low for comfort. Agni rolled down his sleeves, as he sat down on the settee.

'Please wait. Ma'am will be with you shortly. Would you like to have something to drink... tea or coffee?'

'Thanks, I'm fine. I'll wait.'

The girl walked back down the stairs.

Agni's eyes went back to the table. He could spot lipstick marks on the numerous cigarette stubs and on the edge of the whiskey glass. Rituja was obviously stressed for some reason. It was a little past four in the afternoon, too early for the heavy drinking.

Agni needed to know Rituja's schedule for the week. When he texted her earlier in the afternoon mentioning he had not been able to reach her secretary, she informed him that her secretary had taken the rest of the day off and Agni could come down to her bungalow. Agni jumped at the opportunity, thinking he would finally have time to discuss the case with Rituja. He had several questions for her.

Agni heard a door open behind him. In no time, the room was permeated with the familiar musky aroma. Agni turned around to find Rituja walking down the lounge in wobbly steps, the diaphanous pink pallu of her saree barely covering her breasts. Her eyes were glazed. Her hair cascaded down her shoulders, bare except for the thin straps of her blouse. Her saree sat low on the curve of her waist.

'Hey Agni, so good to meet my knight in shining armour again!' Rituja slurred, only too happy to settle down on the same settee at less than an arm's length from Agni. She picked up the unfinished whiskey. 'Care for a drink, Agni?'

Agni refused with a polite nod.

'Oh! You must be on duty, aren't you?'

Agni smiled.

Rituja took a gulp of the drink and lit a cigarette.

'So, what brings you here?' her breath reeked of alcohol. 'You did mention... I don't recall now...,' she said apologetically.

'I would like to know your schedule for the week, Ms Bose. I called your secretary but couldn't reach him,' Agni explained the purpose of his visit, trying to look away from the inebriated Rituja, an eye covered almost completely by her tresses, unabashed desire conspicuous in the other, her saree threatening to slip off her shoulder any moment.

'Oh yes! You did mention,' Rituja stamped the cigarette stub into the ash tray and stood up with some difficulty.

'Let me get my diary...' she tottered towards the bedroom.

She stopped after entering the bedroom. Supporting herself against a wall, she turned towards Agni. With lust writ large upon her face, Rituja allowed her saree to touch the floor, revealing her breasts that almost spilled out of her skimpy blouse. The pendant buried in her cleavage and her waist chain shimmered in the last rays of the setting sun that seeped in through a window Agni could not see. Her deep navel, bared before Agni's unbelieving eyes, seemed to be begging for attention.

Agni stood up and paced across the lounge. He stood at the doorway as Rituja unfastened a hook of her blouse, her breasts rising and falling in rhythm with her heavy breathing. Her eyes were locked with Agni's, silently challenging him to make his move.

Agni pulled the bedroom door shut with a bang right on Rituja's face and turned around.

As he ran down the stairs, anger and dismay took over him. Over the years, his fascination for the woman upstairs had come from her being enigmatic, being completely beyond the reach of lesser mortals who could only fantasise about her. For the fanboy in Agni, she was real, yet she belonged to a different world. A few minutes back, the screen goddess transcended the virtual barrier between their worlds when she looked pleadingly at him, seeking a few minutes of physical gratification.

One moment Agni asked himself why he had taken up the case, the next moment he wanted to run upstairs, shake the intoxicated woman back to her senses and ask, 'Why, oh, why?'

Chapter 19

'So, you have a theory?' ACP Bardhan asked Agni and exchanged glances with DCP Upadhyay. The other officials in the room looked expectantly at Agni.

'I do, sir. What struck me right from the beginning is the obsessive behaviour of the stalker. I read through the e-mails Ms Bose had received at intervals of few weeks. In each of those e-mails, the sender poses as a man of considerable affluence. A banker or a merchant or a celebrity not willing to reveal his identity—you get the drift. The man writing the email professes his love for her, wishes to meet her in private and makes alluring propositions. He talks about taking her along on a luxurious cruise, or investing his fortunes in her movies, or holidaying on private islands, or even of marrying her. The pattern is the same.

'The sender of these emails, assuming for a moment they are from the same person, comes across as someone taking pleasure in setting up a bait for Ms Bose, and waiting to see if she falls for it. In fact, I noticed that contrary to what Ms Bose told us, she had actually replied to the first couple of those emails, expressing her interest in the men and their offers. She became alert when the pattern started repeating at regular intervals.'

'You mean to say, someone has been subjecting her to some kind of test, checking how easily she gives in to temptations?' ACP Bardhan asked Agni.

'Exactly, sir! Now, come to think of the calls. Why is it that this person calls her only at her land-phone at odd hours in the night, and then disconnects the line without saying anything after he hears Ms Bose respond? Why doesn't the stalker call her on her mobile phone?'

DCP Upadhyay spoke this time, 'To check if she's home!'

'Exactly! That's what I think too, sir,' Agni smiled.

'As for the break-in, it was meant to be on a day she was out. The stalker never intended to harm Ms Bose. The person wanted to get into her house and carry out a discreet search of her belongings, looking for clues to whatever Ms Bose is being suspected of,' Agni explained further.

'Brilliant, Agni!' DCP Upadhyay exclaimed. 'This makes a lot of sense. It's not a random stalker, but someone Rituja knows. Someone close to her, possibly a lover, who's insecure and suspicious.' He looked around the room and asked, 'Who's she dating these days?'

'I've already been gathering information from some of her close associates—well, the very few that she has in the industry. There is, indeed, substance to the rumours that she has been dating a cinematographer by the name of Abhishek Roy for a while now. The security guards at her bungalow have also seen him visit her on a number of occasions. The timings of his visits don't seem to suggest that those were business meetings!' Agni brought the DCP up to speed with his findings.

The DCP kept looking at Agni for a few seconds. Then he asked, 'So how does this piece of information help us?'

'Well, there is widespread rumour in the industry that the two of them have recently broken up, though neither of them has come out in public either confirming or refuting the rumours.'

Chapter 20

Present day

Their car turned a corner and hummed down a narrow alley off the main thoroughfare. Agni had always known about the nondescript watering holes in the northern fringes of Kolkata. Those places very often came in the news for all the wrong reasons—brawls, shootouts and prostitution.

However, he had never heard of The Nook, which apparently served as the haunting ground of the rich and the famous when they wanted to let their hair down without compromising on security and privacy. The club was tucked away in a corner of the city, far from the milling crowds of onlookers.

The car was slowing down. Agni could see a fairly long queue near the entrance. However, Rituja's chauffeur seemed to be heading towards a more discreet entrance on the side. Agni could see dark figures gathered around the doorway.

'Looks like the paparazzi got wind of your Friday night plan after all,' Agni quipped. 'We need to be careful.'

'I don't have the faintest idea how they get to know every time!' Rituja looked worried.

'You may not know, but most of them are paid to keep their eyes on you all the time, and follow you wherever you go,' Agni said.

The chauffeur stepped out of the car and walked towards the back door and opened it for Rituja. Agni stepped out on the other side and from the corner of his eyes, could see a bunch of photographers bolt towards their car with their cameras raised high.

Rituja and Agni were greeted by blinding flashlights. Agni ducked and instinctively passed an arm around Rituja, feeling the cold bare skin of her upper arm, pulling her through the heavy door held open for the star guest by a couple of beefy bouncers.

Agni could hear the photographers shouting outside, resenting the easy entry of the celebrity guest, even as the heavy door closed behind them. The noises outside were replaced by the heavy thumping of the bass inside.

Agni was suddenly conscious of Rituja still nestling against him and withdrew his arm. Rituja looked into his eyes and smiled coquettishly, streaks of blue and yellow lights lighting up her face. There were strategically placed mirrors all around, making the club look more spacious than it really was.

'Follow me,' she whispered as Agni felt her hand slip inside his, tugging at him.

Agni could see heads turn as Rituja smiled and waved at some of the revellers she seemed to know. He realized that they were headed towards what looked like a bank of private booths at the far end of the club, making their way through the stamping and swaying crowd on the dance floor.

Rituja moved a curtain aside and Agni saw Mayank Kapoor sprawled on a sofa. For a brief moment, all the advertisements in print and hoardings Agni had seen him in, flashed before his eyes.

Mayank was in a very tight tee and skinny jeans. He reclined on a sofa; his arms stretched along the back at right angles to his sculpted body. He had a mop of shoulder-length hair, which also covered his brow and his right eye. On the table in front of him there was a plate of *kebabs* and a glass of whiskey. He jerked his head, making a futile effort to shift his hair off his eye, and looked up at Agni and Rituja with droopy eyes.

Sitting next to him on the same sofa – unusually close – was a strikingly fair-skinned man with locks also growing past his shoulders, dressed in a loose floral shirt and matching floral trousers. His eyeballs protruded behind designer spectacles, his nose looked botched, and his cheeks were round and flabby in contrast with his lean frame. Agni immediately recognized him as Rocky Chowdhury, the fashion designer who had recently shot to fame with what Agni considered rather garish, bordering on outlandish, designs for men. For instance, Agni could never imagine himself in a fitted navy-blue blazer, unbuttoned to reveal his bare sculpted torso, paired with an orange silk *lehenga* – spectacles with circular frames and red glasses, and ankle-high pink sneakers completing the look.

'Ritu!' Mayank almost screamed and wobbled to his feet. Agni realized he must have been drinking for a while now. He tottered forward from behind the table and hugged Rituja, and then flashed a smile at Agni, extending his hand.

'Mayank, let me introduce ACP Agni Mitra, unless you already know him,' Rituja looked at Agni over her shoulder, 'and who doesn't know Mayank?'

'Of course,' Agni smiled, 'From the highways to our drawing rooms—Mayank Kapoor is everywhere these days!'

Mayank bowed his head, clearly enjoying the adulation.

Rituja then turned towards Rocky, who had already stood up. Agni noticed that Rocky was several inches shorter. 'How are you doing, love? Looking fab as always!' he said as he hugged Rituja. The two made pouts, blowing kisses into the air, as they rubbed cheeks with each other. Once they had disengaged, the designer cast a quick glance at Agni and spoke in Rituja's ear, making sure Agni heard him, 'You sure have one helluva dishy friend, babe! You two seeing each other?'

'Not exactly,' Agni said before Rituja could speak, 'I am here to meet Mayank Kapoor in connection with an investigation. Thanks for the compliment, by the way!'

'Oh, how boring!' Rocky made a face and turned towards Mayank, 'I will make a move, babe! Have to be on an early morning flight to Mumbai tomorrow. I'll call you as soon as I am back in town.' Rocky made a gesture with his thumb and pinkie, and walked out of the booth with an exaggerated swing of his hips.

Mayank had already gone back to the sofa.

He gestured at Rituja and Agni to take up seats. Rituja sat next to Mayank, Agni sat facing them across the table.

'What would you like to drink?' Mayank looked enquiringly at Agni. 'I don't need to ask Ritu. I know what's her poison.'

'Whatever you are drinking,' Agni kept it simple.

Rituja moved the curtain aside and gestured to a waiter, who after taking orders returned shortly afterwards with whiskey for the men and a pink-coloured cocktail for Rituja in a salt-rimmed glass.

Mayank took a long gulp of the drink and looked into Agni's eyes, jerking his head again to shift his hair that got in the way, this time with some success.

'So, what brings the cop here?' Mayank's lips curled in a smile as he drummed on the table.

Rituja inched closer to Mayank. She held his hand and said in what Agni thought was an almost apologetic tone, 'Baby, Agni is investigating the murder of Hiya, and I have told him about Hiya and you...' Her voice trailed off.

Mayank jerked his hand free and looked at Agni.

'So, I'm a suspect now, am I?'

He drained his glass and looked incredulously at Rituja. 'Can't bloody believe this!' He yelled at her, 'I thought you knew how to keep a secret! She's dead, for god's sake!'

He hid his face between his palms and for a few minutes, rocked back and forth. He then stood up and swiftly moving the curtain aside, made his way out of the booth.

'He is very upset over Hiya's death. He's been like this for days now!' Rituja volunteered to explain Mayank's odd behaviour, rather unduly as Agni thought. He found their camaraderie rather interesting. She bent forward to pick up a piece of kebab from the plate, offering Agni a generous view of her bosom above the low neckline of her pink bodycon, a shiny pendant nestled in her cleavage.

Agni looked away, but not before Rituja's eyes had caught his. The flirtatious smile was back on her face.

There was an awkward silence inside the booth. The bass thumped loudly outside.

Mayank was back after a while, carrying a freshly filled glass of whiskey. Agni's eyes went to the open fly of his trousers. Rituja gestured to Mayank, alerting him to his oversight. Mayank promptly zipped himself up.

Back on the couch, he took a sip of the whiskey and looked up at Agni. For a fleeting moment, Agni felt he looked nervous under all that put-on arrogance, as he started drumming again on the tabletop, his legs jerking to his rhythm.

Agni said, 'Mayank, get this clear. You are *not* a suspect,' he paused and added, '*yet*. I am here for a conversation, to know you better.'

Mayank sucked hard on his cigarette and said, 'Okay, let's talk then. Let's get to *know each other*.'

'You have been endorsing the properties of the Chauhans for... how long?'

Mayank closed his eyes, dragging on his cigarette, thinking hard. 'Must be more than two years now. I came down to Kolkata from Patna and was looking for work. The agency put me through to the Chauhans. In fact, one of those advertisements on TV got me my first mega serial on telly.'

'I believe you are now working in a movie.'

'I am.' Mayank looked smug. 'All these Bengali girls love me in the serials, I'm told!' He winked at Rituja. 'So, the same production house decided to give me a break in their latest movie.'

'And you continue to work with the Chauhans?'

'No... not anymore. I... I'm focusing on the movie right now.'

'Do you visit Manav in the hospital?' Agni asked.

Mayank looked tense and restless. He took another generous sip of the whiskey. The drumming on the tabletop was back. So was the jerking of his legs.

'I did go to the hospital... the day after the... the incident. Manav was unconscious.'

'And did you go back afterwards?'

'No... I've been busy. I told you,' Mayank sounded impatient.

Rituja interjected, 'Yes, Mayank is working hard on the movie.' Agni realized that Rituja was trying to show Mayank off in his best light.

'Hiya and you were in a relationship. How did *that* happen?' Agni looked Mayank straight in his eyes.

Mayank reached for his pack of cigarettes and pulled out a stick. He fumbled in his pocket for the lighter, and after he finally found it, he managed to light after a couple of failed attempts. He took a long drag and threw his head back, running his fingers through his unruly hair, shifting the mop off his face.

There was silence inside the booth, interrupted only by the loud music outside.

'We *were* seeing each other.' Mayank finally spoke, his eyes closed. Agni watched him intently. Not a muscle twitched on Mayank's face.

Agni cast a darting glance at Rituja and asked, 'This was before her marriage, I believe?'

'Yes,' Mayank's head hung low and his voice was almost inaudible. Agni was suddenly worried he might fall asleep.

Mayank continued to speak almost in whispers, 'Hiya had been going on and on about Manav not having time for her, about her feeling lonely and needy... I had wanted to make her happy, to spend time with her... and we fell in love. She was ready to break off her marriage with Manav!'

'Then why did she still go ahead and get married to Manav Chauhan?'

'How the fuck do I know?' Mayank yelled, the suddenness of his reaction taking the other two by shock.

He stood up again and walked gingerly to the door. He threw the curtain aside and barked orders for another round of drinks.

He returned to his seat and continued, 'Manav found out about us... dropped by at her set one fine day and took us by surprise. There was a scene... a nasty one... in front of the unit.' He hid his face in his palms. 'I was drunk... very drunk. I was out of my fucking senses. I was very rude with Manav... I... I should've watched my words. That woman... that woman was playing with my mind... bringing out the worst in me...'

'Didn't Manav talk to you after that incident?'

'He... he didn't. I don't blame him. I was very rude with him... I told you. He wanted to break off the engagement...'

'Wouldn't that have been convenient for the two of you?' questioned Agni.

'Yes, yes, yes... but...' Mayank's fingers curled into a punch that landed on the tabletop.

'But...?'

'But Hiya was not willing to let him go, you see. He was *the* Manav Chauhan! It didn't take her too long to change her mind and get into her wedding trousseau! Who the fuck am I?'

Rituja rubbed his back and ran her fingers through his hair, now forming a curtain around his face which was hidden in his palms, as he sat stooping forward. Agni had his eyes fixed on Mayank. The man was hurt, and angry. It would not take a lot for that rage to translate into an uncontrollable desire for revenge.

Mayank went on, 'She must've apologised to Manav... must've begged and pleaded... must've told a bundle of lies... must've said it was I who had seduced her... must've said it was just a stupid fling... and Manav must have given in. He must've realized he had not been paying enough attention to his fiancée... lost in his work! Just as he used to ignore that other girl, he broke up with... what was her name?'

'Neha?'

'Neha... yes, the one he had broken up with before he met Hiya.' Mayank banged the table once again and looked up at Agni, 'But you know what? It wasn't a fling for me! It wasn't, for god's sake!' He almost shouted.

A potent pause and then Mayank continued, 'And... and Manav stopped calling me! I felt like shit... he was my friend goddammit! I owe everything to him... I was very rude with him... I was out of my senses...' Mayank went on mumbling. 'All because of that girl!'

Rituja whispered, 'We know baby... Hiya fucked you up... completely! You didn't know what you were doing!'

Agni noticed from the corner of his eye, the waiter had been waiting outside with the drinks and food, hesitating to step in. Agni moved the curtain aside, gesturing to the waiter to serve.

Mayank took a sip of the drink. That seemed to calm him down somewhat.

'They got married and within days, *this* happens!' Mayank said sadly.

'It must've been hard for you!'

'Fuck... it was!' Mayank yelled. 'I was not in town when they got married. I had returned a couple of days before the news came.' His eyes narrowed, Mayank looked at emptiness, 'And now the Chauhans have nothing to do with me... and the idea is fucking me up!' Agni noticed genuine grief in Mayank's eyes.

Mayank suddenly turned to Rituja and held her hand, 'Darling, can you two please leave me alone? I don't want to talk about Hiya anymore. Or, about the Chauhans... I'm trying to get over this, you know...' his voice drifted off again.

Rituja looked at Agni. He nodded.

Rituja whispered into Mayank's ears, 'Baby, are you sure you'll be fine? Do you have the car?'

'I do... don't worry 'bout me,' he slurred.

Agni finished his drink. He put his hand on Mayank's shoulder and said, 'Take care... I'm sure everything will be fine.'

For some reason, his own words rung hollow in Agni's ears.

Rituja was on the phone with her chauffeur. 'Rakesh, we're coming out now. Be at the side door. Right now, ok?'

She bent over and kissed Mayank on his cheek, who remained seated motionless.

Several flashes blinded Agni as he followed Rituja into the back of her car. He heard one of the photographers scream, 'Hey, isn't that Agni Mitra?'

He had no idea what the papers would make of his appearance with Rituja, stepping out of a club at that unearthly hour. He slammed the door shut and the car started immediately.

After a few minutes, Rituja said, 'I feel sad for Rocky, you know. He loves Mayank to the moon and back.'

Agni nodded. His guess had been confirmed. He reflected on what Rituja had said just now for a few seconds and asked, 'In that case, how did he cope with Mayank's affair with Hiya?'

Rituja turned towards him and asked, 'What do you expect?' She continued, 'He was shattered. You see, Rocky is very sweet by nature. I have never heard him speak ill of anyone. But he did make an exception for Hiya. He hated that girl. He believed, like many of us, that the small-town bitch had married Manav just for his money. He was sure that she would carry on her affair with Mayank even after her marriage.' Rituja paused and then said with a wicked grin, 'In fact, Rocky and I bonded over our mutual hatred for Hiya.'

Agni realized that it was the alcohol talking. Rituja had never opened up about her true feelings for Hiya. He also realized that there was a good reason why Rocky might have wanted to see Hiya dead. Agni made a mental note to ask Arya to keep an eye on the movements of the celebrity designer once he was back in the city, and also to check the details of his phone calls around the time of Hiya's murder.

Rituja had clammed up and turned her face away, realizing probably that she had let slip more than she should have.

After a few minutes, the awkward silence inside the car was broken by the chauffeur. He looked at Rituja in the rear-view mirror and asked, 'Home?'

'Yes, Rakesh. And can you please turn on the radio? It's too quiet in here!' She looked sideways at Agni with a sarcastic smile.

Trucks sped past the car at regular intervals, ferrying idols of Ma Durga to the pandals, accompanied by the frenzied beating of the *dhaak*.

Agni looked at Rituja, streetlights sweeping across her face, the musky aroma of her body wafting inside the car, her breath smelling of alcohol and he was transported in time to the back seat of another car, with the same woman next to him in a similarly intoxicated state more than a decade back — younger and arrogant, with her newly tasted success.

Chapter 21

Ten years back

'Agni, I want you to accompany Rituja and personally supervise the security arrangements. She is very jittery today,' ACP Bardhan waited for Agni's assent, which took longer than he had expected.

'I believe that her own security personnel, along with the armed constables we have deputed, are doing a fine job!' Agni tried to wriggle out of the assignment. The reluctance in his tone was not lost on the ACP.

He tried to figure out why Agni's enthusiasm in the assignment had suddenly ebbed.

'What's the matter with you? You don't seem to understand the fact that this is not one of her closed-door shoots! This is a public event. Half the city will be at the venue. We will have a tough time managing the crowd. Unless we are vigilant, the stalker can sneak in any time and cause harm to her. Rituja herself is aware of the possibility, and she is very worried. She has called me thrice since morning, asking specifically for you!'

Agni had been avoiding Rituja since his last visit to her residence. And now, he would have to accompany her to the awards function at the insistence of the ACP. Agni wondered why she had been asking for him specifically.

***

Agni stood at an arm's length from Rituja as the flashlights blinded him. Rituja flaunted for the press the two trophies she had won

77

earlier in the evening for her brilliant portrayal of a college girl taking up cudgels against her family and the society and giving birth to her daughter, conceived out of wedlock. Readers of the popular movie magazine had voted for her as the best actress of the year, and so had a panel of judges, comprising of eminent movie critics, directors and writers.

The reporters fought against one another for her bites. Rituja had had a few too many drinks at the after-party and talked a dime a dozen, rattling off clichéd answers. Agni looked at his watch, wondering when the farce would end.

'Ma'am, what do you have to say about your ex-lover, Abhishek Roy, citing trust issues as the reason for your recent break-up?'

Agni was suddenly alerted by the question from one of the reporters. He did not know about Rituja, but he himself had not seen that one coming! The next moment he realized that, the seasoned actress, by now, must be adept at handling personal questions from the media. He looked up at Rituja, waiting with bated breath to find out how she reacted to what had so far been the subject of hushed speculations in the gossip mills.

She opened her lips a couple of times, trying perhaps to find a befitting response which, however, eluded her. The suddenness of the question had clearly unsettled her. And she was probably too drunk to let her thinking mind come to her rescue.

She clutched Agni's shirt sleeve. And then, in an act that would be remembered and discussed for years, she stuck her middle finger at the reporter and tottered away with Agni, the cameras going berserk over her receding frame.

Chapter 22

Agni pushed Rituja into the safe confines of the rear seat of her car and slid in next to her, shutting the door with a bang. He gestured to her chauffeur. The car roared to a brisk start and sped off with a deafening screech, to the chagrin of the reporters who started following them, welding their cameras and microphones.

Agni looked at Rituja, streetlights sweeping through her face, the musky aroma of her body wafting inside the car, her breath smelling of whiskey which had already kicked in, her mouth spouting the choicest of abuses, directed at the press.

Her head dropped to a side and landed on Agni's shoulder. The next moment, she inched closer and snuggled against him, her long fingers clutching his shirt at his chest. She raised her head. Her eyes, struggling to stay open, were fixed on Agni.

'Listen... I am sorry about... about what happened the other day in my room... I was out of my mind,' the whiskey fumes in her breath assaulted Agni's nostrils as Rituja nestled on his shoulder.

'Abhi and I were supposed to have lunch after our shoot... and he didn't turn up that morning. The entire unit kept waiting for him. Then, one of the boys in the unit said someone had seen him entering the Oberoi Grand with Avantika earlier that morning. Everyone had been talking about them for weeks, but I had refused to pay heed to the rumours. I believed Abhi was mine.' Rituja paused. Agni could feel the warmth of her tears on his shirt.

'But that afternoon, I wanted to find out for myself. I went to the Grand and then, straight up to his room. The bitch... the very same one everyone had been talking about... opened the door wrapped in just a bedsheet... and I saw Abhi inside the room scurrying for cover. That bastard! He has the balls to say he has trust issues with me!' Rituja screamed.

Agni could see the chauffeur's eyes darting frequently to the rear-view mirror.

Rituja's grip on Agni's shirt tightened.

'I was shattered, Agni. My world came crashing down. I broke down... I made a fool of myself in the hotel... I kept asking myself why Abhi did that to me. The only answer I could find was that he didn't find me attractive anymore... that I couldn't satisfy him in bed anymore...' Rituja was now howling.

'I realized that fame isn't such a big deal after all... that at the end of the day, I'm just a girl looking for love... you know, that famous Julia Roberts line from... from Notting Hill... I realized that was my truth... every girl's truth. I rushed home... I started drinking like there was no tomorrow... I was expecting you that afternoon,' Rituja looked into Agni's eyes. 'I don't know what came over me... I suddenly had to prove to myself that a man—any man—would find me attractive... that I would be able to make his iron resolve melt by revealing my body before him... that he would pounce on me... tear my clothes away and have wild sex with me... and all you did was...' Rituja suddenly started laughing, '...you shut the door on my face and walked away... just as Abhi had done! That hurt Agni, that hurt a lot!' She wept.

Rituja had flicked open the top button of Agni's shirt and her fingers stroked his chest hair. 'Look into my eyes, Agni, and tell me you don't find me attractive,' she whispered, her warm breath fanning his face.

'Please get a hold on yourself, Ms Bose.'

'Tell me Agni... in all these days, was there never a moment when you wanted to touch me... to fuck me...?'

'You are not in your senses, Ms Bose,' Agni said through his clenched teeth.

'Kiss me,' she said throatily as her nails dug into Agni's chest, her lips landing on his.

Agni held Rituja by her shoulders and pushed her away.

'Stop the car,' Agni shouted at the chauffeur, who promptly followed his order.

The car screeched to a halt. Agni stepped out of the car and slammed the door shut. He buttoned up his shirt, the scratches Rituja had left on his chest burning.

'You'll have to pay for this, Agni,' Rituja screamed, pushing her head out of the window. Agni looked into her eyes and the madness he saw there made his heart skip a beat.

***

Agni stood before ACP Bardhan. He had hardly slept the night before, after the showdown with Rituja in her car. Every time he closed his eyes, he saw her face, contorted with unbridled lust and then with spiteful rage on being turned down. He had seen her eyes spewing venom, staring back at him from the speeding car.

'I never expected this from you, Agni! Rituja called me this morning. I am told there was a security violation during the event yesterday!' ACP Bardhan was beside himself with anger.

'None that I am aware of, sir,' Agni replied nonchalantly.

'Exactly her point! She feels you are not being vigilant enough. She told me that there was someone who had groped her last evening after the awards function, and none of the armed constables was anywhere nearby. You were nowhere near her! She is feeling very insecure. This doesn't make us look good, Agni!'

'Sir, I was with her everywhere she went last night,' Agni resisted the urge to add 'but for her bedroom' and continued, 'and so were the armed constables. She is imagining things! People often start hallucinating when they are too scared of something or someone.'

'For god's sake! That's the worst explanation I've ever heard, Agni!' The ACP fumed, banging on his desk.

Agni did not want to drag the conversation.

'So, what are your orders for me, sir?' Agni looked into the ACP's eyes.

'I can't allow you to continue with this assignment, Agni. I need to take you off before this gets any worse. As I warned you earlier, Rituja has contacts in all the right places.'

'I don't doubt that,' Agni muttered under his breath.

He turned around and walked out.

Rituja had exacted her revenge. This would probably be an indelible scar on his career, Agni thought.

He would never forgive, or forget, that woman!

***

Two weeks passed by. Agni was yet to get over the bitterness he felt over the unprecedented turn of events.

He was in bed when the phone rang.

When he picked up the receiver, he heard ACP Bardhan at the other end of the line.

'Agni, have you seen the newspapers this morning?' The ACP asked.

'No, sir. Anything that needs my attention?'

'I called you to say that you have a sharp mind, indeed! I really appreciate.'

'What's this about, sir?' Agni sat up straight. He was taken aback at the change in ACP Bardhan's demeanour. The ACP had hardly spoken to him over the last couple of weeks.

'Your theory about the stalking was proved correct last night, Agni. Take a look at the papers!'

The ACP ended the call.

Agni immediately got out of bed and walked up to the balcony. He picked up the newspaper and went to page three.

There was news about the birthday bash of a Tollywood starlet. Rituja was present in the party when Abhishek Roy, her ex-lover who had accused her of adultery while he himself had been dating a model, turned up drunk. He reportedly started screaming at Rituja, blaming her for their break-up a month back. Completely uninhibited, thanks to his drinking, he said he had email evidence to prove that Rituja had agreed to sleep with wealthy businessmen willing to fund her projects or offering to take her on holidays to exotic destinations, or showering expensive gifts on her, while she had been in a relationship with him. He further said, on most nights, when he had called Rituja, she had not been home, spending time probably with her suitors. They fought frequently, and their relationship turned sour. When Rituja instructed her security staff to never allow him inside or in the vicinity of her house, he broke into her house to discover ridiculously expensive gifts that Rituja had accepted from other men without mentioning them ever to Abhishek in return for, according to him, sexual favours. Rituja's complete lack of commitment at a time when they had been planning to settle down, drove him to walk out of the relationship. He decided to rub salt on Rituja's injury by adding that he had since then chosen to sleep with every woman who had thrown herself at him, with a vengeance—including Avantika, the same woman with whom Rituja had found him inside a room in the Oberoi Grand.

As he finished reading the report, Agni looked at the busy streets outside his balcony. The city went about its business, completely oblivious to the trials and tribulations of the men and women it worshipped on the silver screen.

He allowed himself a smile after a very long time and headed towards the shower. He looked forward to going to work after a long time.

Chapter 23

Present day

Sleep eluded Manav Chauhan as he lay on the hospital bed. He had a throbbing headache, brought over by the tormenting images that had ravaged his sedative-induced sleep a while back. However much he resisted, his mind drifted to another time, another place.

He found himself transported to Hiya's van at a shooting location in Kolkata a few weeks before their wedding. That was Hiya's last schedule before her break. Manav had been very busy and had hardly found time for Hiya over the last few days.

Hiya had just finished shooting a few dance moves for a song when Manav turned up around noon. There was a break before the next shot, which would see Hiya in a different costume, dancing to the same number. Hiya gestured to the make-up artist to wait and let Manav in.

'Is everything alright? I almost convinced myself that you don't remember me anymore,' indignation rang loud in Hiya's voice, as she picked up a towel and turned on the air conditioner.

Manav was slumped on a leather couch inside the van, his blazer off, his tie loosened. He was struggling to find words to explain what he did realize had been an unpardonable blunder. There had been days in the last week when he had not called her even once. And the wedding was just a couple of weeks away. Hiya had every right to be cross.

'You know how my schedule is, don't you? And then, we had the architects flying down from Singapore with the designs...'

Manav made a half-hearted attempt at salvaging the situation. Hiya did not let him finish.

'You don't love me anymore,' she declared. Manav remembered he had heard that line before, from another woman. Hiya sounded almost like Neha. Most certainly because he had been equally callous.

Hiya stood up and made her way towards the shower as tears welled up in her eyes. Manav got up and hugged her from behind, stopping her in her tracks.

'You know that's not true, don't you?' Manav nestled his face on Hiya's neck and whispered, the warmth of his breath fanning the back of her ears. He kissed her on the neck. Hiya suppressed her moan with some effort and she had goosebumps all over her arms. His touch felt electric, his cologne intoxicating. A part of her was angry with him as he had been ignoring her for days, and another part of her wanted to melt in his arms in gay abandon that very moment. What was happening to her? That was not how it was supposed to be! For days, she had been planning to take Manav to task the next time they met. For days, she had rued over the fact that Manav had perhaps started taking her for granted already. She freed herself from his arms, but the fire still coursed through her veins, her breathing was still laboured.

Manav ran his fingers through his hair and returned to the couch. Hiya moved into the shower cabinet, without bothering to shut the translucent door behind her.

Hiya untied her hair. She had her back to Manav as she unzipped the knee-length scarlet dress at the back and let it drop to the floor. As she stepped out of it, Hiya had no clue what had come over her. Her pulse raced as she slowly turned to face the half-closed door of the shower cabinet in her purple lacy bra and skimpy panties, her hair cascading down her shoulders, her eyes locked with Manav's. As her hands reached back to unclasp her bra, Manav walked across the van nodding his head with a smile on his lips and a glint in his eyes. As he tried to shut the door of the shower cabinet, Hiya flung the bra outside and grabbed him by the collar. She pulled him inside and planted her feverish lips on his, her pent-up anger giving way to raw earthy passion. Like a woman famished, she drew blood from Manav's lower lip, her warm supple breasts caressing Manav's hard chest, her fingers making their way through his hair.

Manav pulled himself free. He took her in a hug and kissed her on the forehead.

'Not before the wedding, remember?' he smiled. 'Don't make it difficult for me, sweetheart.'

'I know... I know, Manav! But I missed you so much! I thought it was all over between us!' tears streamed down her flushed cheeks, as Hiya clutched his shirt. She looked up at his face and smiling through her tears, she said, 'But every time you say that, you sound so sweet! It makes me fall in love with you all over again. It makes you so special, so different from everyone else and our wedding night such a special night to wait for!'

Manav liked the fact that Hiya respected his decision. Neha used to find it 'old-fashioned'. Manav kissed her on the cheek and hugged her.

As Hiya was about to go back to the shower, there was a loud knock on the door of her van.

They looked at each other.

'The make-up artist?' Manav asked.

'I don't think so. I told him I'd call him when I was ready...'

The knocks grew louder, each more impatient than the earlier.

Hiya put on a robe. Manav opened the door of the van.

'Ah, what a surprise!' Manav exclaimed as he saw Mayank standing outside, his tee drenched in sweat, his eyes barely visible under his messy locks.

'Surprise, indeed!' Mayank remarked in reply, his breath reeking of alcohol. He was drunk and could barely stand straight. 'Look who's here!'

'Mayank, what're you doing here?' Manav demanded.

Mayank did not bother to answer. He stood on his toes and peeped inside.

'Mayank, I asked you a question,' Manav's voice climbed a notch.

Mayank jerked his head backward, shifting his locks off his eyes, and looked at Manav in the eyes.

'Manav,' he smiled, 'do you want me to answer that question, or, do you want to ask your fiancée? In fact, you can ask the guys here, in this unit, if you want to spare your sweetheart the trouble.' Manav saw that half the unit had gathered close to the van. It seemed the unit was not surprised to see Mayank.

Manav turned around. Hiya stood right behind him. The colour had vanished from her face.

'Manav, I can explain this! It's not... it's not how you think...' Hiya mumbled.

Mayank did not let her finish. 'Really?' he slurred as he walked towards the van in wobbly steps, 'In that case, I'd like to know myself what *you* think is going on!' He glared at Hiya. 'Just because your fiancé decides to make a surprise visit after ages, you don't know me anymore?'

Mayank pulled out a hip flask. He took a swig of the drink and rubbed his mouth with the back of his hand. He tottered closer to the van and whispered conspiratorially, 'Tell me, sweetheart, are you wearing that purple lace lingerie like you promised to me?' He turned towards Manav and said, 'Manav, remember her photoshoot for *The Calcutta News* last Saturday? She promised me she would wear the same purple lingerie the next time we met. Oh, maybe you don't have the time for reading tabloids. 'Coz if you did, this wouldn't have come to you as a surprise. Those journos have been writing about *us* for weeks now.' Mayank cracked up. He was clearly out of his senses. That was not the way he normally spoke to Manav.

Manav grabbed Mayank by the collar of his tee, his teeth clenched, his rippling muscles threatening to burst out of his shirt sleeves.

'Take it easy, Manav,' Mayank was unperturbed as he grabbed Manav's wrists setting himself free, 'Maybe she's a wee bit too hot for you to handle.' Mayank winked, followed by an obscene laughter.

Manav shoved him away, his face contorted in disgust.

He turned towards Hiya. She was sobbing, her face hidden in her palms.

'I've got all my answers, Hiya. I know what colour you are wearing today for your lover. You should have thought twice before showing it off to me!' Manav grabbed her by the hair and brought his face menacingly close to hers. He said, 'This is it! We're over!'

As he stormed away, he could hear Mayank laughing like a maniac even as Hiya kept calling out Manav's name between her sobs.

***

Manav opened his eyes, his fingers clutching the hospital bedsheet, sweat trickling down his face. The memories were disturbingly fresh and refused to stop chasing him. He was tired. He could not run any faster.

Chapter 24

In another part of the city at that very moment, Agni was wide awake inside his study. The commissioner had called in the evening. He had wanted to meet Agni the next morning.

Agni finished his coffee in one long gulp and started going through the notes he had made over the last several days while talking to a number of individuals who had been close to Hiya Sen.

Balaram Sen, Hiya's uncle
Burdwan

On Hiya's career in the movies:

'Sir, I struggle to make ends meet. Yet, I never compromised on her education. She was a brilliant student. I thought she would take up a job and take care of the family. I have no idea how she was bitten by this bug. She did not want to complete her studies. She wanted to go away to Kolkata. I tried to reason with her. She was in no mood to listen and we fought every day. But she did run away eventually. She started modelling and within a few months, started acting in movies. Made quite a name for herself! We saw her pictures in the newspapers, magazines and on the posters that were put up all over the town. No one in our family had ever been a public figure, sir. And that too, so popular! There were long queues in front of the ticket counter when her movies released.

How did I feel? Well, one moment I felt proud. The next moment, I felt ashamed when I heard people say dirty things about the industry and about her. Some of the neighbours made obscene speculations about how she had made her way to the top so fast. But, sir, I brought her up with my own hands! How could I bring myself to hate that girl? Also, I have to tell you this. She never forgot to send us money. Not a single month! She also visited us a couple of times. There was a stampede in front of our house the second time she came. I went to Kolkata once to meet her. She took me to the sets. A different world altogether! She looked happy. And that's what mattered to me.'

On Hiya's marriage to Manav Chauhan:

'Sir, to be honest, I had never heard of him. Hiya called us and said she was getting married to a businessman. Her aunt wasn't too happy about the fact that he wasn't a Bengali. He was successful, wealthy and very popular in Kolkata. Well, it was her life. We didn't have a say. We were happy that she was happy.

No, we couldn't attend her wedding. Her aunt was not well, and I chose to stay with my wife. She called us in the morning and said she would send a car to get us. But, we couldn't make it.

No. Manav never had anything to do with us.'

On Hiya's death:

'Sir, I read about it in the papers. The news came on television. No one from that family bothered to call us and inform! We were shattered. Her aunt fell ill. For two days, she couldn't get out of bed. I couldn't even go to Kolkata to see my little girl, as I had to be with my wife. The neighbours wouldn't let us mourn in peace with all kinds of filthy gossip.

I heard they had beaten up Manav badly. You've arrested three boys, have you? I read in the papers. Sir, can you please tell me what exactly happened? I'm so confused. And I don't want to call her in-laws.'

Surinder Chauhan with his wife in attendance
Kolkata

'Why are the police bothering us again? I've already given my statement!

You are exploring fresh angles to the incident? What's there to explore? This city is becoming increasingly unsafe with every passing day! There's complete breakdown of law and order! Go out on the streets and do something concrete instead of wasting your time sitting here in my air-conditioned room and talking and talking!'

On whether he wants justice for Hiya:

'Let me be very honest with you, ACP. All that I want right now is to have my son back home — hale and hearty. My boy has an empire to run!

This is the misfortune that girl brought on our family! I've no idea what had come over Manav. He would have been very happy with Neha. What a nice girl!'

On what he felt about Hiya:

'What can I say about Hiya? It was her business to seduce the audience in provocative dresses and tasteless dance moves. This was inevitable! I had always warned Manav that he should stay away from these types of girls!'

On his son's future:

'I had given my word to Deepak, but Manav didn't bother to respect it! He ended up paying a heavy price. Neha visits him every day in the hospital and takes care of him, in spite of what he did to her. I hope and pray that my son realizes his mistake and the two of them get together. That would make everyone happy. It feels like the curse on our family has finally been lifted!'

Aniruddha Goswami, Director
Kolkata

On his movie with Hiya and Rituja:

'That movie is very close to my heart, ACP. It is about sibling rivalry—two sisters who compete with each other for everything all through their lives, finally falling in love with the same man. They would stop at nothing to get what they want, even if it means they go down the path of self-destruction.'

On the unique casting:

'The casting is the USP of my movie. Everyone knows that Hiya did not share a great rapport with Rituja. The rift between them was mainly due to professional reasons. I thought that their real-life rivalry would get translated into outstanding performances on screen with each one of them trying her best to outdo the other.

No. The movie is not shelved. I am making changes to the script to accommodate the unfortunate circumstances. But I will complete this movie at any cost.'

On what the movie meant for Rituja:

'The movie is extremely important for Rituja. As you may be aware, she hasn't exactly been very successful in the recent past. But look at her career spanning more than a decade! She has given us so many memorable movies. This is just a bad phase — happens with the greatest of performers. She will definitely bounce back with my movie!'

On the conflict between his heroines:

'Well, the two heroines had their differences, and I was aware of what I was getting into when I cast them. While my intention was to play on those differences to extract their best on-screen performances, it was getting difficult handling their off-screen clashes.'

On the ugly fight between Hiya and Rituja on the sets:

'Yes, we did have a nasty scene on the sets one day. It got widely reported. We had called over a few reporters to cover the shoot. It was an important sequence in the movie, which involved both the heroines. The idea was to get some media coverage with photos from the sets. What happened instead was outrageous!'

On Hiya's reaction:

'Hiya did complain to me about Rituja, saying she wouldn't be able to continue working in the movie with her. Suggested I should look for another senior actress who did not hold a grudge against her because of her success. I told her I would consider her suggestion. In any case, she was going on a long break for her wedding. I thought by the time she came back, things would have cooled off and both the actresses would have come round.'

On Rituja's reaction:

'Did I tell Rituja? I did, actually. I told her to control her temper. I told her there were differences between her style of working and that of the new crop of artistes. I also made a subtle mention of the fact that her chips were down at the moment, and my movie meant everything to her. Having Hiya in the movie would, in fact, guarantee a good opening at the box office.

No, I don't think she was too happy. I've known Rituja for years. She has always been used to having her own way on a movie set. And she refuses to accept the fact that times have changed. That newer actors have moved far ahead. She fumed and fretted for days!'

On his experience of working with Hiya:

'Well, I'll be very candid with you, ACP. Especially because this has to do with a murder investigation. I found Hiya's behaviour in the days leading to her marriage rather odd.

Come to think of it. She was a girl who came from nowhere and scaled enviable heights of fame in almost no time. She was among the most coveted actors in the industry. The audience loved her. She hadn't tasted failure anytime in the recent past. In this movie, she had the opportunity to prove her acting chops in a face-off with one of the most famous actresses of our industry. On the personal front, she was engaged to one of the most desirable bachelors in town.

I had expected her to be bubbling with energy, with enthusiasm. Instead, all through the shoot, she was just the opposite. It seemed she had completely lost interest in her work. That's what Rituja interpreted as her lack of professionalism. She was never on time. She called in sick rather frequently. She forgot her lines. She frequently went blank during narrations. She looked exhausted. She was depressed. I had no clue what was wrong with her. But there was definitely something gnawing away inside her.

Yes, I did hear there was a spat involving her between Manav and the guy she had started dating weeks before her wedding. I thought that was weird! Don't you think so? Why did she get into that fling? We'd never know I guess.'

Avik Sinha, Hiya's Secretary
Kolkata

On Hiya's behaviour in the days leading to her wedding:

'To tell you the truth, sir, she was not her usual self. I had no idea what had come over her. She kept cancelling shoots and refused to take calls. The producers were after me. She would be in a foul mood most of the time. We fought a few times. I was trying to make her see sense. I couldn't help wonder at times if success had gone to her head. Have seen that happen to some of the big names in the industry. But I did figure out that it was something else.'

On Hiya's rumoured affair with Mayank:

'Well, there was truth in that rumour, sir. She started hanging out with him with just a few weeks to go for her wedding. I wasn't happy about it. The media didn't take kindly to the affair either. I felt she was toying with her life. She was clearly going through an emotional turmoil. At times, she was happy. Especially when she was with Mayank. And there were times, when she was depressed and aloof. She was confused. I didn't see much of Mr Chauhan around her during that phase, either. I thought that was strange! And that fight on the sets between Mr Chauhan and Mayank did not help! She got a lot of bad press.

Well, I guess she sorted herself out at the end. We were very happy when she came around and married Mr Chauhan.'

Chapter 25

The commissioner was lost in thought, his fingers anxiously tapping on the table, his forehead creased. Agni had finished reporting his findings and his theories a while back. Arya had his eyes fixed on the commissioner.

He finally looked up.

'Guys, I appreciate your hard work. Must say you've covered a lot of ground in a very short time. But, pardon my saying this, the case now looks more complicated!'

'It does, sir. If those three men were indeed hired for the job, which I personally feel is what transpired in reality, we now know a number of persons, who either had very strong motives for the crime, or, stood to benefit from the death of Hiya Sen.'

'I agree.' The commissioner left his chair and walked up to the window that opened to an uncharacteristically grey autumn sky outside. 'But these are still theories, Agni.'

'I don't deny that. I also understand that our investigation will hit a roadblock unless we can catch hold of Asif bhai, who picked up the contract, or, gather more substantial evidence to back up any of our theories for it to be admissible in the court.'

'I am sorry to say that we've seen no progress there.' The commissioner walked back to his desk. 'No one has a clue yet about Asif's whereabouts! I've been following up with Interpol regularly. Most of what you just narrated are conjectures—very plausible, but we will need more concrete evidence to support any of those conclusions.'

'Sir, prosecution will be asked to produce evidence in support of the theory of contract killing,' Arya reminded the commissioner.

'Yes, I know! But we don't have anything on our hands at the moment!' The helplessness in the commissioner's voice was not lost on the others in the room. 'One hell of a situation!' he continued. 'In the present scenario, we will need to underplay the suggestion of this being a paid job. We will look like a bunch of idiots if we hold up that theory and then, cannot trace the origin of the money trail. It serves us better to stick to the theory of this being an impulsive act of retaliation by those three anti-socials in the aftermath of the brawl in the bar. I don't want you to waste any more of your time on this case. There are other, more pressing demands that need your attention.'

Agni did not reply. There were theories that crowded his disquieted mind, even as a sense of despair at the stalemate gnawed away at his heart.

He picked up the day's newspaper and scanned the front page. The world had got busy with newer acts of decadence. There was no dearth of violence to accompany our morning tea. In a matter of days, Hiya Sen's death had been relegated to an inconspicuous corner of the fifth page.

Chapter 26

Two months later

Lakhan Sahu stepped gingerly out of a run-down shanty inside one of the slums in Tiljala.

The abject poverty of slum dwellers in Tiljala formed a sharp contrast with the luxurious lifestyle of occupants of the skyscrapers that had come up in the neighbourhood. Most of the slum dwellers were employed in the tanneries in the area. They had been joined back in the day by a refugee population from the neighbouring Bangladesh. The slums today formed a virtual haven for an increasingly large number of disreputable elements in the city.

Lakhan had moved out with his family to a rented house in the neighbourhood from one of the slums in the area a couple of months back, after his release from the hospital. However, he still had friends in the slum, and would drop by every Saturday night to indulge his addiction to cheap country liquor.

Tonight, he chose to overstep his self-imposed limits on how much he would usually drink. He had reason to celebrate.

As he tottered down a narrow lane cutting through the ramshackle houses on both sides, the chill in the air made him shiver. He wrapped his worn-out shawl tightly around his sparse frame and supported himself by reaching out to a nearby wall. The cold silence of the night was interrupted only by the occasional shrieks of hungry infants inside the shacks or the prolonged mournful wails of street dogs.

As Lakhan turned around the bend of an alley, the hooded figure stepped out of the shadows. It moved in brisk silent steps behind Lakhan as he hummed an undecipherable tune, walking in unsure steps, his hands perpetually looking for support. The world around him was a blur.

By the time Lakhan realized he had company on those sleepy alleys, there was a strong arm around his neck and the warm breath of his aggressor fanned the back of his head. With his free hand, the assailant pulled out a knife tucked into the waist of his trousers at the small of his back. Lakhan opened his mouth trying to breathe, but the man had cut off the supply of air to his lungs with Lakhan's neck firmly in his grip. The sharp edge of the knife glistened ominously in front of Lakhan's protruding eyes as he flailed his arms helplessly, his muffled throaty cries lost in the racket made by a pack of dogs fighting over leftovers in a nearby garbage bin.

Their cacophony reached a crescendo even as the cold steel blade of the knife made a swift, terminal slit across Lakhan's neck. Within seconds, the blood started spurting out and Lakhan dropped to the ground, writhing in agony.

The man waited as long as the spasms swept through Lakhan's sparse frame.

When he was finally convinced that the body sprawled on the ground at his feet showed no sign of life, the man tucked the knife back into the small of his waist and started walking in the direction of the highway.

He stopped in his tracks and looked one last time at his victim.

'Who would have imagined the old bugger had so much blood in him?' he muttered to himself as the mist engulfed his receding figure.

Chapter 27

Agni picked up the morning newspaper as he sipped his coffee.

All through the autumn, when the city erupted with festivities, when happy faces beamed all around and laughter echoed in the autumn air, when crowds thronged streets awash with lights, Agni was alone, holed up in his flat. He was conscious of his loneliness more than ever—that's what the festive season did to him.

He got busy with two other cases with lesser and lesser time for the Hiya Sen murder, but could not get the case out of his mind. He was irritable and angry with himself, as he spent night after night trying to fit the pieces of the puzzle together, failing to make headway. It seemed to him that all the clues were in front of his eyes, but they simply did not fit together into a logical whole. And the sounds of the dhaak and the crackers drifting into his twelfth-floor apartment did not help.

The three offenders were still in custody. There was still no trace of Asif bhai. Manav Chauhan had been released from the hospital and was back on page three! There were pictures of Mayank Kapoor walking the ramp for Rocky Chowdhury in a recent show. There were advertisements announcing that China Valley would open its largest outlet in Kolkata in the Town Centre Mall, Manav's newest shopping mall in the Salt Lake area. Everyone seemed to have welcomed the reconciliation between the Chauhans and the Awasthis. Rumours were rife that Manav and Neha were seeing each other again. The song Agni had seen being picturised on Rituja and the newcomer was being aired on television channels. Rituja expectedly drew flak from the media not only for the suggestive moves and the skin show, but also for having no choice but to romance considerably younger actors. It was rumoured that leading actors now refused to work with her and that they opted for younger heroines they could bank on for ensuring a bigger opening at the box office. A producer notorious for sleazy movies had announced his next project with Rituja and Mayank Kapoor.

The world had clearly moved on, but Agni lived in a time warp. His frustration over the complete lack of progress in the Hiya Sen murder case over the last several weeks was uppermost in his mind when he opened his eyes every morning. He went through his copious notes again and again. He classified his suspects into two categories. The murderer could be someone who stood to gain materially from Hiya's death, or someone who had a more emotional reason to see her dead. All of them had very strong motives. Any one of them could have hired the killers through Asif bhai. All of them roamed free.

He had been skimming through the pages of the newspaper, his mind clearly elsewhere, when his phone buzzed.

It was Arya.

'Agni, good morning. I have news!' Arya sounded excited.

'Shoot,' Agni put the newspaper down.

'Lakhan Sahu was murdered last night!'

Agni sat upright.

'Where are you calling from?' asked Agni.

'We are in a slum at Tiljala. Lakhan was found dead in an alley here. Throat slit. He was out drinking last night with his friends in the slum. The officer-in-charge called me up because of Lakhan's connection with Hiya Sen's murder. I think you should be here.'

'I'll start right away,' answered Agni.

Agni felt as if the world around him, hopelessly frozen for what seemed like ages, had suddenly found life in yet another death, as if a giant machine had suddenly whirred back to life from its slumber.

Chapter 28

Lakhan's lifeless body lay spread-eagled across a clearing that led to dingy alleys meandering through rows of shacks inside one of the biggest slums in the Tiljala area. He had a woollen cap on. A shawl he had wrapped himself with was spread out on the dust. He made a gory sight, his mouth gaping, his face contorted with the pain and the shock he must have gone into in his last moments with imminent death staring him in the face. There was a deep gash through his throat, around which the blood had caked. He wore a printed kurta and a half-sleeve sweater over it, both of which were soaked in blood. The blood had coursed down to his cotton pants. There was a rubber slipper on one of his feet. The other slipper from the pair lay upturned about a foot away from his body. There was a garbage bin close by. A dirty gutter, filled to the brim, ran right next to where Lakhan lay. The stench was nauseating. Flies buzzed around the body. The forensic experts had a tough time keeping the dogs at bay as they went about their job.

'Who would have thought the frail, old man had so much blood in him?' that was the thought uppermost in Agni's mind when he looked at the body.

He got down on a knee and looked for signs of scuffle. He could find none—no bruises, no scratches. It was just that deep gash that had taken Lakhan's life. That was all that the murderer had wanted. Agni was told that Lakhan's mobile phone had been

104 | Sourabh Mukherjee

found in one of his trousers' pockets. Lakhan still had his purse in his hip pocket. The murderer had no interest in his money.

'Which one is *his* house?' Agni asked Arya, looking at the rows of shacks.

'He did not live here, Agni. He moved with his family to a rented house away from the slum a couple of months back, after his release from the hospital.'

'Do we know why he was here last night?'

'He used to come here every Saturday to drink with his buddies. He was attacked on his way back home last night.' Arya informed.

'Who identified him?' Agni asked.

'His friends who live here in the slum found the body. His wife was also brought here. She identified him.' Arya filled him in.

Agni stood up and looked at his watch. His eyes went to the stretch of the Eastern Metropolitan Bypass at a distance. He could barely make out Deya, the five hundred-feet-high aerial skywalk between the twin towers of The Atmosphere at a distance. The morning mist was still thick.

'I would like to meet his family,' Agni said as he made his way out of the slum.

Chapter 29

Agni stood in front of the distraught woman, who stopped wailing as soon as she saw him. A girl clinging to the woman looked up at Agni with wide eyes. Tears had dried on her cheeks. Agni assumed she was Lakhan's daughter. One of the women who were busy consoling Lakhan's wife shifted her attention to the visitor in the room.

'I'm sorry about this, but I have to ask you a few questions. This won't take long.' Agni sounded apologetic, realizing all over again how much he hated having to dispassionately question the recently bereaved kin of a murder victim.

Lakhan's wife nodded.

'When did you see him last?'

'Around ten last night. After that, he went out drinking. I used to tell him not to venture into that slum so late in the night, but he wouldn't listen.' The woman spoke under her breath, bursting into a fresh bout of tears.

'I believe you stayed in that slum till a few months back. When exactly did you move to this house?'

The woman made silent calculations. Then she said, 'About two months back. After he came back from the hospital. We came into a lot of money. We paid off all our debts and moved into this house.'

The revelation took Agni by surprise. 'Do you know where all that money came from?' he asked.

'I've no idea. I never asked him.'

'Do you know any of his friends in the slum? The ones he met every Saturday night?'

'I know quite a few. All of them are crooked! I asked him to stay away from them, but he wouldn't listen! The worst among them was Asif bhai! I was scared of him. He gave me the creeps!'

The hair rose on Agni's neck.

'Did Lakhan know Asif bhai?'

'Everyone knows Asif bhai! He rules this place! *He* used to suck up to Asif bhai and I hated him for that!' The emphasis meant she was referring to her dead husband.

'Do you know where Asif bhai is now?' Agni kept his fingers crossed.

'No idea. I was happy when he left the place.'

'When did Asif bhai leave?'

'Around the same time when *he* was admitted to the hospital.'

'Was he still working with the Chauhans?'

'He wasn't. He left that job, sir.'

'Really? When did he leave that job?' Agni could not conceal the surprise in his voice.

'A few days after we came here. He took up another job. He said that the pay was better.'

'I see,' Agni was deep in thought.

'We were very happy. The money was good. He was also saving money for our daughter, but good times don't last.' The woman sobbed.

Agni looked around the room. There was a study desk stacked with books in one corner. There was a wooden table with a television set on it. He could see a set-top box and a DVD player. He could spot a small refrigerator in the kitchen. Lakhan was making money, no doubt.

'He was so happy last night!' the woman cried out loud, beating her forehead with her rickety hands.

'Anything special about last night?' Agni asked.

'He said he had received a lot of money.'

'You do *not* know where that money came from, I assume?'

'No, I don't know. I didn't bother to ask ever! He took good care of us and that's what mattered!' she sobbed while sounding defiant of her ignorance of the source of money the family had been living on. 'I thought it was the new job he had taken up.'

Agni realized there was no point in questioning her further.

'If you remember anything or want to tell me something, call me on this number.' Agni scribbled his number on a piece of paper and handed it to her.

Agni met Arya as he stepped out of the house.

'Anything useful?' Arya asked.

Agni put on his shades and headed towards his car.

'He came into a lot of money about two months back when he paid off his debts and moved to this house. That was around the time Hiya was murdered. He then took up a new job,' Agni sounded excited as he continued, 'Go inside that house, Arya. You'll see signs of suddenly acquired prosperity, unexpected of someone in his position. It can't be just his chauffeur's job! We will need to check his bank account.'

He stopped in his tracks and added, 'And, he was close to Asif bhai!'

Chapter 30

Arya's excitement was palpable as he walked into Agni's office. Agni was going through Lakhan's autopsy report.

Lakhan's clothes were soaked in blood, especially on the front aspect. A few defence injuries had been detected on the forearms. A cut-throat injury in the form of a deep, gaping incision was present on the front aspect of his neck. The wound had cut through the skin into the left jugular vein. The wound was directed from left to right, with greater depth on the left and trailing off to the right. This suggested that the assailant had attacked Lakhan from the back and with the right hand, inflicted the wound on the left side of Lakhan's neck.

No other external wounds had been detected on other parts of the body. After overall consideration, the cause of death had been attributed to 'shock and haemorrhage as a result of cut-throat injury caused by a hard and sharp-edged object'.

Agni looked up from Lakhan's autopsy report and gestured to Arya, offering a chair.

'Agni, I have news for you!'

'So it seems, indeed. Did you check Lakhan's bank account?'

'Yes, I did! Guess what? Lakhan made three deposits of hefty sums of money in his bank over the last couple of months. Eight weeks back, around the time of Hiya's murder, he deposited a sum of fifty thousand. A month after that, another twenty-five thousand. On the day of his murder, he deposited another twenty-five thousand. There were monthly deposits of more reasonable amounts, presumably from his wage, as well. All deposits in cash, made by Lakhan himself.' Arya informed Agni.

'I guessed as much. There can be only one explanation. Lakhan was blackmailing someone!' Agni got up from his seat and paced up and down the room, his arms folded behind him. He stopped and turned towards Arya. 'Have you checked the call records of his phone?'

'Yes! There are five numbers used more frequently than the rest over the last two months. One belongs to his wife. There is an outstation number that belongs to his family in Orissa. We have not been able to trace another number. It is a prepaid number and cannot be reached at the moment. We checked details of registration available with the service provider. They turned out to be fake!'

There were creases on Agni's brow.

'I won't be surprised if the number belonged to the person Lakhan was blackmailing. I strongly believe it's that same person who killed him. Lakhan's was the inevitable end of a blackmailer's run of good luck! Of course, you don't expect the murderer to be available now at the number that Lakhan used. Did you manage to trace the other two numbers?'

'Yes, Agni. The other two belong to the family he worked for. In fact, the last call made to Lakhan's mobile that morning was from one of those two numbers. Now, guess who he worked for?' Arya had a grin on his face.

'Someone we know?' Agni sounded impatient.

'Deepak Awasthi! Lakhan left his job with the Chauhans and was hired by the Awasthis. Lakhan had been working for Deepak for about two months before he was murdered. They had no clue as to his whereabouts on the night of the murder, as Lakhan had taken the evening off. The next morning, they tried his mobile a couple of times, and then gave up when they didn't receive a response from him. They came to know about his death when I met them.'

A potent silence descended inside the room. Agni tried to assimilate the fantastic revelation, and its possible implications.

He sat at the edge of his desk and thought aloud, 'Lakhan's purse was intact. His mobile phone was with him. Whoever killed him clearly had no interest in his belongings. The murderer also had knowledge of Lakhan's routine—the fact that he went to the slum every Saturday night and returned home late. This was a premeditated murder, Arya. So, why did Lakhan have to die?

'There is undoubtedly a secret that Lakhan was privy to. Looking at the timings of the payments, that secret surely has something to do with the car-jack and Hiya's murder. I am now more convinced than ever that there indeed was a plot behind Hiya's murder, which was made to look like an impulsive action by a bunch of goons. This means that there was substance, after all, to the theory of Hiya's death being a contract killing.

'Now the question is, what was that big secret that Lakhan knew?'

Chapter 31

Agni paced up and down the room as Arya watched him in awe.

'There are two possibilities here,' Agni said. 'Let's consider the first. Lakhan might have come to know something *while* he was working for the Awasthis, probably soon after he took up the new job. In that case, it is likely that the Awasthis tried to silence him, first by paying him large sums of money at regular intervals starting with the fifty thousand that they paid him around two months back, then two instalments of twenty-five thousand each, and eventually killing him, when his demands became unreasonable, or, they felt otherwise threatened.'

Agni paused and took a sip of the black coffee from his mug on the table. He pushed the mug aside when he realized the coffee had gone cold.

'In the second scenario, Lakhan himself played a part in the execution of that plan and then blackmailed the perpetrator. The Awasthis may have been involved. Or, it could be someone else.'

'So, in the second scenario, are you suggesting that, whoever had hatched the plan had taken Lakhan into confidence? You mean, Lakhan was an accomplice?' Arya asked.

'It is likely. And they agreed that Lakhan would take a few blows himself in the act to ward off any suspicion.' Agni went back to his seat.

'But what role could *he* have played?' Arya wondered aloud.

'Lakhan was close to Asif bhai. It is highly possible that Lakhan acted as a mediator. He might have introduced the perpetrator to Asif bhai. There is another way he could have helped,' Agni smiled, reclining in his chair.

Looking at the quizzical expression Arya had on his face, Agni continued, 'In the choice of a convenient route. I asked you if anything struck you as odd after we had spoken to Lakhan in the hospital, remember? Now let me tell you what I found odd. The Chauhans live in Ballygunge Circular Road. When one is returning from Tipple, which is near the airport, one can choose to drive through the New Town Expressway or take an alternate route over the VIP Road Flyover. Although driving through the Expressway means a detour of almost ten kilometres and it gets deserted late in the night, drivers often opt for this route as it's a more relaxed drive. One can avoid the congestion which is common on the other route. I've been wondering all along that, had the Chauhans chosen the alternate route along the VIP Road Flyover that night, the mishap could have been averted, as that route passes through a busy thoroughfare, even during late hours. You cannot rule out the possibility that the choice, in this case, was intentional!'

'Why didn't Manav object?' Arya questioned.

'This might have seemed to be a trivial decision at that moment. Also, let's not forget that Manav must have been extremely agitated over the incident at the club some time back. His wife was probably trying to pacify him. I think it was hardly the time to pick a fight with your trusted driver of more than five years for his choice of route. For all you know, Lakhan might even have offered a plausible explanation for his decision.'

'Brilliant, Agni!' Arya applauded Agni's deduction. 'Lakhan took a few blows himself, but was paid a hefty sum of money. After his release from the hospital, Lakhan left his job with the Chauhans to distance himself from the family he had betrayed. He paid off his dues and rented a new house. He took up a job with the Awasthis. But his greed got the better of him and he started blackmailing whoever had hatched the scheme. The conspirator paid him on two occasions and then, decided to finish him off!' Arya summed up the tragic turn of likely events.

Agni muttered to himself, 'Someone somewhere is very scared right now, Arya. The killer had no choice but to finish off Lakhan. But when someone knows your deepest and darkest secret, you can never be sure if that person had let a few others in on that secret. Lakhan's death may not mean that the secret is buried forever, and the killer knows that too!'

Chapter 32

Agni could sense a general air of gloom as soon as he stepped inside the office of Awasthi Restaurants Pvt Ltd. Deepak Awasthi's office was at the far end of a passageway which had rooms on both sides. Most of the rooms were empty, even at the peak of business at eleven in the morning, which Agni felt might be because the occupants of those rooms had been let go.

Agni walked into a large, square room that was Deepak's office. Deepak was sitting behind a messy desk. There was a shelf behind him, with trophies that had gathered dust. The carpet needed cleaning, and the air-conditioner made so much noise that Agni had to raise his voice as he greeted Deepak.

'Good morning, Mr Awasthi,' said Agni as he pulled a chair and sat down, facing Deepak.

'Good morning,' Deepak said, not sounding very cheerful. He cast a glance at the air-conditioner and asked, 'The damn thing needs servicing. Do you mind if I switch it off for some time while we talk?'

Agni was relieved. He was in no mood to torture his vocal cords. After the air-conditioner had come to a halt with a thud, Agni did not speak for a few seconds, as if reluctant to break the soothing silence, which had suddenly descended on the room. He finally spoke.

'Mr Awasthi, you must be aware that your chauffeur, Lakhan Sahu, was brutally murdered a couple of days back.'

'Most unfortunate. He was a good man,' Awasthi said, shaking his head. He then hastened to add, 'I have already spoken to an Inspector who visited me.' Deepak seemed to imply that he was not sure about the purpose of Agni's visit.

'Yes, you did,' Agni said, 'you did mention to my colleague that Lakhan had been working for you over the last two months. That was around the time he was released from the hospital, wasn't it?'

Deepak sat up straight at the mention of Lakhan's hospitalization. 'Yes, that was an unfortunate incident, too,' he said.

'It was. I understand that the Chauhans are like family, and Lakhan had worked for them for many years before he left the job. Is it fair to assume that you had known Lakhan before he started working for you?' Agni had looked into the call records of Lakhan's mobile phone, and the dead man had had several lengthy conversations with Deepak Awasthi around the time of Hiya's murder.

Agni noticed that Deepak's casual demeanour had completely vanished. He looked alert, concentrating on every word that Agni spoke.

'Yes, I had known Lakhan for a long time. He had driven for me in his free time on a few occasions when my previous chauffeur had not turned up on some pretext or the other.'

'Why do you think he left the Chauhans?' Agni asked, his eyes fixed on Deepak.

Deepak squirmed on his seat and said, 'I have no idea. I guess we will never know. Maybe it was guilt.'

Agni bent forward and asked, 'Guilt? Why do you say that?'

Deepak realized that the wrong word had slipped off his careless tongue, and the cop would now latch on to it. He took the next few seconds to gather his thoughts. Then he said, 'That was just my assumption! He might have blamed himself for what had happened on that fateful night. He could have taken an alternate route. He could have noticed the bike following the car. He could have fought the goons – who knows, he might have blamed himself for so many reasons!'

Agni nodded, not pushing that line of questioning any further. Instead, he asked, 'Did you pay Lakhan a hefty bonus or lent him money anytime in the last two months?'

'Why do you ask?' Deepak sounded somewhat agitated.

'You didn't answer my question,' Agni said.

'No... no, I never did!'

'Did you know that Lakhan lived in a slum in Tiljala and knew certain nefarious elements from that area?' Agni asked next.

'I did know that he lived in Tiljala,' Deepak pulled out a handkerchief and wiped the sweat off his brow, 'but I don't consider it my business to keep a tab on who my servants and drivers hang out with after work!'

Agni smiled and said, 'I think you must, the next time you hire a chauffeur! After all, Lakhan drove your family around.' He paused briefly and said, 'Talking of your family, you must have had a hard time when Mr. Chauhan called off his marriage with your daughter?'

Deepak emptied the glass of water on his table and said, 'I don't know what any of this has got to do with Lakhan's murder. But I will still answer your question. The only thing that matters to me is the smile on my daughter's face. It was a difficult time for Neha. Manav's decision broke her heart. But I stood by her like a rock and I brought her around.'

Agni nodded appreciatively and said, 'She is lucky to have a father like you, Mr. Awasthi! She seems to be doing fine now. I met her the other day at her boutique. I believe you have been mending bridges with the Chauhans too! At least something nice has come out of an otherwise dreadful tragedy, what do you think?'

Agni saw the colour rising to Deepak's cheeks. He looked away and said, 'The bridges had never been broken, ACP Mitra! And now, if you will excuse me, I have an important meeting to attend.'

As Agni left the room, he heard the air conditioner roaring back to life.

Chapter 33

When Agni was shown into the office of Manav Chauhan, it was close to lunch time. Agni realized that, Manav had a busy schedule, and he probably was not very keen about spending a lot of time with Agni. That consideration must have dictated his choice of the time and the venue for the meeting.

'Good afternoon, Mr Chauhan,' Agni greeted Manav as the later stepped forward from behind his desk and shook Agni's hand.

'Good afternoon, ACP Mitra. It's been a while since we met!' Manav smiled warmly.

'Looks like it's back to business as usual for you,' Agni remarked.

'It is, it is...,' Manav went back to his chair. 'I came back to work a couple of weeks back. There is so much to catch up on! Trust me, the backlog is driving me mad.'

'I completely understand. I promise this won't take long,' Agni said reassuringly.

'Have you made any headway into the investigation, ACP?' Manav kept looking at Agni expectantly, an eyebrow raised, trying to gauge the purpose of his visit.

'Do you know that Lakhan Sahu was murdered a couple of days back in a slum near Tiljala?' Agni did not answer Manav and asked instead.

'Oh yes, that was quite shocking! Neha told me about it. She, of course, didn't have the details. But I've been curious...'

'Someone had slit his throat, rather brutally. Lakhan did not stay in the slum. He had moved to a new house with his family right after he had been discharged from the hospital. He used to visit his friends in the slum every Saturday night. Last Saturday, he was in the slum, drinking with his friends. He was killed when he was on his way back home later that night.' Agni explained.

Manav emptied the glass of water on his table. The details had evidently unsettled him.

'I'm told he stopped working for you after his return from the hospital.' Agni looked at Manav enquiringly.

'Yes, he did,' Manav's eyebrows were wrinkled.

'Did you notice anything unusual in his behaviour at that time?'

'Well, I thought his decision itself was rather unusual. Don't you think so? He had been working with me for more than five years. I lent him money whenever he needed. His family was invited every time we threw a party or celebrated a special occasion at home. We took good care of him and his family during his treatment after the... the mishap. I was very surprised when he said he wanted to leave the job right after leaving the hospital.'

'Didn't you ask him why?'

'Of course, I did. He said he would not be able to continue driving for me. That the memories of that night would not let him concentrate,' Manav paused. 'Then I reasoned with myself that the incident must've been very traumatic for him. At that time, none of us had got over the tragedy. I realized that the tragedy had affected different people in different ways. It must have been difficult for Lakhan to continue working with me, being constantly reminded of that night. He was probably right. So, I didn't really insist.'

'You do have a point there, Mr Chauhan. How did you feel when you found out he had started working for the Awasthis?'

'Well, the Awasthis are like family, and they knew Lakhan for many years. He had always done odd jobs for them in the past, even driving for them at times as a substitute for their regular chauffeur. He didn't have to try too hard to find another job! As for me, I wasn't surprised. In fact, I was happy for Lakhan.'

Agni paused briefly and then said, 'Do you know that Lakhan came into a lot of money around that time?'

Manav bent forward. 'What do you mean?'

'Someone paid him a hefty sum of money. Fifty thousand, to be precise. He cleared his debts and moved to a new house. That's not all. He received large sums of money from someone twice in the subsequent months. Twenty-five thousand, on two occasions.'

'Really? How do you know?' Manav looked confused.

'We checked his bank account.'

'Do you know from whom? More importantly, why?'

'I think he was blackmailing someone.' Agni replied. 'We don't know whom, because every time he himself deposited cash in the bank.'

Agni then went on to explain his theory.

Manav heard him patiently, and then his jaws tightened.

'ACP Mitra, you are entitled to your opinion, but I don't agree with your suggestion that Lakhan might have been involved in a conspiracy to harm us. One could trust him blindly. And, as for your suggestion that the Awasthis had been up to something that Lakhan came to know about while he worked for them and then started blackmailing them, I find that equally preposterous!' Manav paused briefly, and then spoke again, 'In fact, rather outrageous! As I said, the Awasthis are family. You are casting aspersions on several people who are very close to our family and to me!'

'I'm afraid, Mr Chauhan, someone might have taken advantage of your blind faith. For all you know, your trust might have been misplaced. In any case, you are not the first one to have been *taken for a ride*. Well, maybe quite literally in this case!' There was a wry smile on Agni's face.

The pun had not gone down too well with Manav. He did not look amused. He rather looked visibly offended by Agni's suggestions. Agni continued, unperturbed, 'Mr Chauhan, I am now convinced that there was a conspiracy behind Hiya's murder. I've asked this earlier. Do you have any idea who might have been behind this? Do you suspect anyone?'

'ACP, I told you, there is no dearth of my enemies. I guess that's an unavoidable outcome of success! Sometimes, your adversary chooses to hit you where it would hurt the most. Everyone knew how much I loved Hiya.' Manav's voice trailed off. He ran his fingers through his hair.

For the first time since he had walked into that room, Agni realized that Manav still looked weak and vulnerable.

Manav glanced at the clock on the opposite wall behind Agni. Agni took that as a sign.

He stood up and said, 'Mr Chauhan, thanks for your time. If there's anything at all that you want to share with me, or if you manage to remember anything unusual about Lakhan, you know how to reach me.'

'Sure, ACP. I am as eager as you are to get to the bottom of this. Looks like everyone I hold close to my heart is destined to leave me!'

Agni walked out. Manav's closing comment rang in his ears.

As Agni was about to step out of Manav's office, a red Audi halted in the driveway. Neha Awasthi stepped out of the car and made her way towards Manav's office. As they crossed each other, she removed her shades and looked appraisingly at Agni. Agni smiled and bowed his head. Neha did not return the greeting.

'Why are you here again, nosey cop? I thought we were done with you!' Agni could almost read the unspoken question in her eyes.

Chapter 34

Agni locked his car and walked in the direction of Tipple, his hands inside his pockets. He had heard a while back on the FM radio in his car that this was the coldest day of the season so far.

As soon as he walked past the doors of the club, he was greeted by the heavy thump of the bass. It was pleasantly warm inside. The club seemed to be bursting at the seams with the mid-week crowd.

When he looked around, he could spot at least two movie stars, an upcoming fashion model who had been making headlines in the tabloids over the last few weeks for her bold pictures and statements on social media, and a retired cricketer. The noisy and boisterous lot reminded him of Mushtaq, Rishi and Ashfaq. They had come into easy money, which granted them the privilege of hobnobbing with celebrities who frequented Tipple. There was the ubiquitous corporate crowd, desperate to drown the mid-week stress in their tipples. The dance floor, which looked a tad too small from the distance, was packed with frenzied revellers sweating it out as the DJ belted out one chartbuster after another from his console at the far corner of the club.

As Agni took in the sights and sounds inside the club, his mind was transported to the fateful evening when Manav had got into a brawl right inside that club with three men on that very dance floor – the three men who eventually raped and killed his wife. As he looked around, Agni realized that Tipple was indeed a busy club and a lot of eyes must have been on the celebrity couple that evening. Agni had wanted a first-hand feel of the vibe inside Tipple. He also wanted to talk to the manager.

'Welcome, sir!' Kuldeep Singh, the manager of Tipple, approached him with a hand stretched out. Agni shook his hand and then followed him to his office a floor above.

'It's a pleasure to have you in Tipple,' Kuldeep said. Agni was not sure about the reason behind the manager's pleasure— his job, or, his addiction? 'How can I help you, sir?' the manager asked.

'Well, thanks for your hospitality,' Agni smiled and came straight to the point. 'I have a few questions about the night Manav Chauhan and Hiya Sen were in Tipple for the last time.'

Kuldeep suddenly looked very serious and alert. He sat up straight in his chair.

'Sure, sir. I'd be happy to answer your questions. Though I've already spoken to the police and the media about that night...'

'I do understand, Mr Singh. And I must thank you for that. I have a few questions of my own.'

'Of course... please go ahead,' there was a hint of apprehension in Kuldeep's voice.

'I believe Manav Chauhan got into a brawl with three men inside the club that night,' Agni looked enquiringly at Kuldeep.

'Yes! That was very unfortunate, sir. We do try to make sure we don't allow rowdies inside the club. But, you know, how difficult it is these days! All kinds of people with loads of cash to splurge...'

'I completely understand,' Agni did not let him finish. 'How did *you* get to know about the brawl?'

'One of the boys from the security staff came up to my office here and told me. After all, they were celebrity guests!'

'What did you see when you got there?'

'It was madness! The music had stopped. All the tables were empty. People were on their feet, circling around Mr Chauhan and the three guys, who were exchanging blows and hurling abuses at each other! Some of the guests were taking pictures! A couple of boys from the security staff were trying to pull the men apart. Ms Sen stood at a distance. She was scared, almost pale.'

'Quite a scene!' Agni sighed. 'Did you know the three men?'

'The bartender and some of the waiters did. Turned out, they had been regulars here over the last two-three months. Must be the kind who've suddenly come into money. I figured out they had caused trouble on a couple of occasions in the past. Been rude to the bartender and the waiters, made passes at women – you know, that sort of thing. Nothing like what they had done that night, though.'

'Which means that, there must have been a few other regulars among the guests who would also have recognised those three men?'

'Very likely, sir.'

Agni mulled over the plan. If the brawl was indeed a staged act, it had been played out convincingly before a packed audience in an impeccably chosen venue with a celebrity couple and three rowdies, infamous for their prior acts of hooliganism and bullying inside the club. It would be difficult for anyone who had been in the club that night to forget that incident or the men involved. That would only help give away the three men, taking the focus away from the real perpetrator of the plan.

'I believe you have CCTV footages,' Agni checked.

'Yes, we do. I passed them on to the police. I guess that helped in the identification of the three men.'

'Yes, indeed. One more question. Were Manav and Hiya regulars here?'

'They had visited us on a couple of occasions in the past. I wouldn't actually call them regulars.' The manager informed Agni.

Agni reflected on this piece of information. If Manav and Hiya were not regulars, the perpetrator of the staged act had had some way of knowing that they would be in Tipple that night.

This was someone close to them.

Chapter 35

Agni thanked Kuldeep and came down.

When he managed to reach the bar, there were two rows of heads in front of him. He had to raise his voice above the din to order his whiskey.

The whiskey arrived almost at the same time as a paunchy balding man vacated a bar-stool, belching audibly. Agni moved fast and grabbed the seat.

The whiskey soothed Agni's frayed nerves. For the past one week, the police had not made any headway into the investigation of Lakhan's murder. Agni had spoken to Lakhan's neighbours and his friends in the slum, whom he met every Saturday night. All of them had noticed Lakhan's sudden change of fortune, but none of them knew why and how. Lakhan had never let anything out, even during the hooch sessions. They did confirm that Lakhan had been close to Asif bhai, even though his wife was not particularly happy about it. The police had been unable to track the mysterious number that featured prominently in Lakhan's call records. That was probably the person Lakhan had been blackmailing, who had gone into hiding after the driver's murder. Agni believed whole-heartedly in his hypothesis, but he knew he needed substantial evidence in favour of his theory. The money trail Agni had been trying to unearth since the murder of Hiya Sen had only become more complicated with Lakhan's death and the mystery surrounding it.

He was suddenly hurled back into reality by the familiar sound of a woman's laughter. He turned his shoulder discreetly in the direction of the laughter and saw Rituja seated with Mayank in a corner of the club. She continued laughing, her head thrown back. Mayank sat facing her. His hair was tied in a ponytail. He was gesticulating, probably cracking a joke. Agni looked away avoiding their eyes, not in the mood to join the party. He remembered that the two of them were working together in a movie.

However, Agni found himself glancing back at their table every few minutes. The jocular ambience vanished after a while, and the two seemed to be engrossed in a rather grim discussion. Rituja looked flustered and bent over the table, speaking animatedly. Mayank looked defiant and Agni could see him reclining in his chair, nodding his head frequently. As Agni kept looking, he saw the glasses served on the table being emptied with alarming regularity, and Rituja's impatience visibly mounting by the minute. As Mayank got restless, she held his hands in what was clearly a conciliatory gesture.

After a few minutes, something snapped between the two. Mayank stood up and turned around to leave, upsetting a full glass in the process. The drink landed on his trousers and the glass on the floor, instantly shattering to pieces. Those in tables close by turned in the direction of the two. Rituja looked embarrassed.

'Fuck!' Mayank shouted and grabbed a handful of tissues, trying to wipe the drink off his trousers. Rituja stood up, still trying to dissuade him, holding him by his hand. Mayank jerked his hand free rudely and headed for the door, walking past the crowded bar, barely noticing anything or anyone that came in his way. Rituja threw her hands up in despair and gestured to the waiter for yet another drink.

Something was wrong, very wrong, between the two of them!

Chapter 36

The noise on the street was deafening. Photographers and reporters jostled behind the police barricade. It was a very cold winter morning, the sky a depressing dull grey.

The television stations had been reporting the news for a while. The police had a tough time managing the hordes of people, especially the weeping women, who had braved the morning chill and come out on the street. There were others who had stopped on their way to work. Offices of the software companies in New Town were not very far.

There was frenzied clicking of cameras all around – from the long-nosed DSLR cameras of the press photographers to the mobile cameras of the bystanders. They photographed the police vans, the teeming crowd on the street, the five-storeyed Galaxy Apartments, whose entrance was now blocked with tape. The balcony on the topmost floor from where he had fallen was on the rear side of the building, beyond the reach of prying lenses. There were vans with satellite dishes on their roofs, and journalists speaking into cameras, offering all kinds of speculations and comments.

'...from the balcony of his bedroom last night, landing on a car parked in the backyard...'

'...we don't know yet if he was alone when he fell...'

'...forensic experts are inside his apartment...'

The windscreen of the car, parked in the backyard of the apartment complex, had shattered from the impact. Mayank

Kapoor's head had bled into the heavily dented roof of the car. Part of his face, turned to a side, was crushed beyond recognition, his mane spread over his shoulders. The one visible eye had been reduced to a dull white slit. One of his outstretched arms was twisted in a grotesque manner. He was in a white tee and black Bermuda shorts.

Agni walked up to Arya. 'When is the ambulance coming?' he enquired.

'On the way. I hope we'll get rid of the crowd once the body is taken away.'

'What do you think? Did he commit suicide?' Agni looked up at Mayank's balcony adjoining his bedroom in the topmost floor.

'I'm quite sure he did. The guy was unstable. He was drunk most of the time, probably a junkie too! Had no clue about how to handle his sudden and unexpected popularity. Had rich immoral friends who further corrupted him.' Arya dismissed the claim to fame of the departed actor with a gesture of his hand.

Agni remembered the couple of occasions when he had seen Mayank. He remembered the hurt in his eyes when he talked about his failed relationship with Hiya. He remembered his apprehensions about the future of his relationship with Manav and the Chauhans in general, which, in a way, had shaped his career, and which he had jeopardized in a fit of drunken rage, fighting over Hiya. He remembered the pain and frustration that his air of vain arrogance could not hide. He was, beyond doubt, a troubled soul. Agni remembered him walking out of Tipple last night, angry and restless. Did his rendezvous with Rituja have anything to do with the tragic turn of events later in the night?

'What did the doc have to say about the time of death?' Agni asked Arya.

'Between two and four. We may know better after the autopsy.'

'I'd like to take a look inside his flat.'

Agni got into the elevator that took him to Mayank's flat on the topmost floor, now teeming with photographers and forensic experts.

The main door opened to a hall. A sofa set was spread out around a low table. There were a few fashion magazines on the table. There was a television on the wall facing the sofa. On the other wall, there was a picture of Mayank, smiling radiantly, like Agni had never seen him smile when he was alive. Those were the fake smiles hurting souls like Mayank sold to earn their daily bread.

At the other end of the room, there was a dining table and a refrigerator. There was a bone china plate with a few peanuts and a bottle of whiskey that was almost empty.

At the far end of the hall, there was a door that opened to the bedroom. Agni walked through the door. There were pictures of Mayank all over the walls in various moods and poses, and with more famous celebrities in some of the pictures. The bed had not been slept on.

The door to a small balcony adjoining the bedroom was open.

As Agni stood in the balcony looking down at the body on the roof of the car below, he wondered what had been going through Mayank's mind when he had stood on the same spot a few hours back before he had supposedly thrown himself over the edge.

He kept looking intently at where Mayank's body had landed. And then, something struck him.

He took a step back from the edge of the balcony. He then walked back to the edge and looked down again. He made a few mental calculations.

Agni walked back into the apartment. The forensic experts had already cleared out the dining table, taking the plate and the bottle of whiskey in their possession.

When Arya walked into the apartment after a while, he saw Agni frantically pacing around. Agni had gloves on and was moving in and out of rooms, opening cupboards, looking into shelves and pulling out drawers. He finally started crawling on the floor on all fours, peeping under beds, sofas and tables.

'Agni, what do you think you are doing?' Arya did not try to conceal his surprise, bordering on amusement, at Agni's incomprehensible behaviour.

Agni stood up, looking very worried. 'Arya, I want our experts to verify this. But, as per my calculations, if Mayank jumped from that balcony, he would have landed several yards short of that car,' he declared, without bothering to answer Arya's question.

'What are you suggesting?' Arya asked, as his eyes narrowed.

'I have a feeling Mayank did not jump from the balcony. Someone pushed him down.'

Chapter 37

There was silence inside the room, as Arya tried to weigh the implications of what Agni had just suggested. What had looked like a simple case of suicide just a while back, had suddenly taken an unexpected turn.

Agni spoke again.

'Arya, you asked me what I was looking for. Can you imagine someone in this day and age not using a mobile phone? Or, a computer, for that matter?'

'Of course not! What are you now getting at?' Arya looked confused.

'There isn't a single mobile phone in this apartment. I know there isn't any with Mayank either, as that's one of the things I checked at the outset!' Agni's finger pointed downward. 'And no laptop or tablet either. Don't you find that unbelievable?'

'Well, it does look odd!' Arya muttered.

'It sure *is* odd!' Agni exclaimed, 'And the only explanation can be that there was someone in this apartment who removed everything!'

A chill went down Arya's spine. 'And why would anyone do that, leaving out all the other valuables?' he asked, looking around the apartment.

'Consider this. What could be there in mobile phones or in a laptop or in a tablet that one might want to hide from the world? I am thinking messages, pictures, favourite websites, documents.' Agni explained, as he paced up and down the living room.

He turned towards Arya and said, 'Arya, it won't be difficult to find Mayank's mobile phone number. We need to check call logs. I know Mayank was with Rituja last evening. I need to know who else our Kapoor boy has been talking to lately.'

Agni looked at the dull grey sky outside. He said, 'If Mayank Kapoor had a visitor last night, his neighbour next door might know.'

Chapter 38

When Agni knocked on the door of 'P. K. Samaddar', as the nameplate proclaimed, it was opened by a frail emaciated man with glazed eyes and very little white hair. He looked clearly dismayed at the general commotion around him.

'Yes?' he asked.

'I am ACP Agni Mitra and this is my colleague Inspector Arya Sen. We wanted to ask you a few questions, Mr...'

'Samaddar, Pradip Kumar Samaddar,' the man announced. 'I always knew the lout will bring the police to my door some day!' Agni was taken aback at the rather blasphemous reference to the dead.

'Please come inside,' Mr Samaddar told the two policemen and walked into his flat with a slight limp. Agni and Arya followed him to the sparsely furnished living room.

Agni came straight to the point.

'Where were you last night, Mr Samaddar?'

Mr Samaddar's eyes narrowed. 'What? Am I a suspect? Just because I live next door?' He almost shouted.

'Not yet. But being the next-door neighbour of the deceased, you might have valuable information if you were home last night.' Agni explained.

'Of course, I was home! I don't spend my nights outside drinking with loose men and women like these guys do!' He pointed in the direction of Mayank's flat. His indignation with Mayank Kapoor's lifestyle was evident.

'Let's not get personal here, Mr Samaddar. So, I understand you were home last night.'

'Yes, I was,' Mr Samaddar replied. The sternness in Agni's voice had somewhat mellowed him down.

'Did you see or hear anything unusual?' Agni asked.

'Unusual? There was nothing usual about that man!' Mr Samaddar's fury had been rekindled by Agni's question. 'He came in late every night. Drunk, on most nights. And his friends! Loud, boisterous, outrageously dressed! He played music loud late into the night! A number of residents signed a petition against him and submitted to me a few weeks back. Well, just so you know, I am the chairman of the cooperative. That guy was an antisocial element!'

'I understand. Now, about last night...'

'He came home drunk as usual. I heard sounds and looked through the peep-hole. He was fumbling for the key, as usual. Shut his door with a bang. Then, for quite some time, there was no sound from his flat. Coming to think of it, he was rather quiet last night! No loud music, no maniacal laughter on the phone. I went to bed and fell asleep.' Mr Samaddar stopped speaking momentarily, and then continued, 'And then, I was suddenly awakened. I heard loud voices in his flat. It seemed as if he was shouting at someone.'

'What time was it?' asked Arya.

'It was around half past two.'

'How can you be so sure about the time?'

'I have an alarm clock on the bedside table. I get up at six every morning for my morning walk,' answered Mr Samaddar, 'I checked the time when the noises from his flat woke me up.'

'Did you hear anyone else in his flat? You said it had seemed to you that Mayank had been talking to someone.'

'No. I could only hear Mayank shouting! For all you know, he might have been speaking on the phone.'

'Could you make out what he was saying?'

'No. My hearing is not at its best these days, I'm afraid.'

'I do understand,' Agni paused to think and then asked, 'Did you hear the crash when Mayank fell down?'

'I did! I was awake. Also, the car alarm went off when he fell on the roof of the car.'

'What did you do when you heard the crash?'

'I went to the balcony immediately. I saw him...' Mr Samaddar closed his eyes. 'What a ghastly sight!' he shivered. He paused briefly, trying to regain his composure, and then continued, 'The security guard from the night shift was there too. He was screaming. The lights had come on in many of the flats. People had heard the crash and the car alarm, and had come out in their balconies.'

'What did you do next?'

'I came back inside and rushed out of my flat. I looked at Mayank's flat. The door was closed. Just as I had seen it last. Then I went down.'

'Who did you see when you went down?' Agni asked.

'Apparently, I was the first one to have gone down. The security guard was there, of course. We were joined before long by the owner of the car, who was followed by many of the other residents.'

'Who informed the police?'

'I did.'

'Did you hear anyone inside Mayank's flat after the crash? Did you hear anyone leaving?'

'No. I didn't hear anyone inside his flat after the crash.'

Mr Samaddar thought for a while and said, 'Do you think there was someone else in his flat last night? Your questions seem to be suggesting that possibility. Well, even if there was someone inside the flat, the person might have left when I was in the balcony of my flat. I was too shocked to register anything. Also, if someone left Mayank's flat without making a lot of noise, the sound would not reach my bedroom balcony.'

'Do you stay alone here, Mr Samaddar?'

'Yes. My son is in the United States. Wife passed away last year. Heart attack...'

'That would be all, Mr Samaddar. Sorry for the trouble.'

'That's alright, ACP. I'd be happy if I can be of any help.' It seemed that, the importance of the recently concluded interview had finally dawned on Mr Samaddar. Agni thanked him and walked out. Arya had finished taking notes and he joined Agni. Agni's head was lowered, his brows wrinkled. He looked engrossed in his thoughts. He suddenly stopped and walked back to Mr Samaddar's flat. He knocked on the door again.

Mr Samaddar opened the door.

'What is it now?' he asked, his irritation ringing loud in his voice.

'Mr Samaddar, there's one more thing I need to ask you,' Agni sounded almost apologetic. 'How did you go down after you had heard the crash? Did you take the stairs, or, did you go down by the elevator?'

Mr Samaddar kept looking at Agni for a few seconds, trying to gauge the significance of that question. 'I took the elevator,' he replied after some time.

'When you pressed the button on the elevator, did it come up, or was it already on this floor?' Agni asked.

Mr Samaddar promptly replied, 'It was on the ground floor. I remember I was frustrated as I was in a hurry. I pressed the button a couple of times. I couldn't wait for the elevator, and almost thought of taking the stairs. But my gout pain had got worse since last week.'

'Thanks again for your time, Mr Samaddar,' said Agni.

As he made his way towards the elevator with Arya, Agni was lost in his thoughts.

Chapter 39

The office of the security guard next to the entrance of Galaxy Apartments was small and stifling. One could enter Galaxy through a barred iron gate that opened to a parking space, which led to a lobby area from where one could take an elevator to the floors above. The guard Arjun, was seated on a stool. A register with records of visitors moving into and out of the apartment complex was open before him on a table. There was a small ceiling fan that remained switched off during the winter months.

Agni stood outside the security post, accompanied by Arya, whose pen was poised on the notepad ready to take down notes. Agni noticed to his dismay that there was no CCTV surveillance in the complex.

'How did you get on with Mayank Kapoor?' Agni asked, 'You probably saw a lot of him.'

'Well, I would see Mayank sir go in and out past my post,' Arjun said. 'He didn't talk much. Maybe just a "Hello" if our eyes met. In any case, expecting someone to say "Please" if he has to request me for something, and to thank me when there is a reason to, is much more than what I expect from most people living in these flats.' He made a sweeping gesture at the flats with his hand. 'So, his cold behaviour did not matter to me, especially when you consider the fact that he was a *star*,' Arjun added, stressing on the last word. Agni thought that was a rather flattering compliment for someone who had recently made the transition from television serials to low budget Tollywood movies.

'Longest chat we ever had was about the difficulties of staying away from home and missing home-cooked food. He was an immigrant in the city like myself, you know.' Agni did not miss the tone of solidarity with the departed model in Arjun's voice.

'Can you tell us what happened last night?' Agni asked. 'Mentioning the time wherever you can.' For a fleeting few seconds, images of Mayank Kapoor leaving Tipple, drunk and agitated, flashed before Agni's eyes. That must have been around ten-thirty last night.

'Let me see,' Arjun ran his fingers through his grubby long hair and then continued, 'Mayank sir came in around quarter past eleven. He was drunk and had been banging loudly on the gate. When I opened the gate, I saw that he had come by a cab. I let him in and the taxi left.'

'Do you remember the number of the cab, by any chance?'

'No, sir. I hardly noticed,' Arjun smiled sheepishly.

'It's alright. I understand,' Agni reassured him.

'Does the main gate remain locked at night?' Agni asked next.

'Yes, sir.'

'You have the key?'

'I do. In fact, they all do, sir, the residents. They can open the main gate with their keys, walk across the parking space, and take the elevator to their flats. If one has a visitor during the night, one has to call me for allowing entry.' Agni noticed a telephone set inside the security post.

'So, why did you have to *let him in* last night? I'm assuming Mayank Kapoor had his own key to the main gate.'

'He did. I don't know about last night, though. Also, he was drunk. He kept banging on the gate.'

'You didn't ask him why he hadn't used his own key?' asked Agni.

'No, sir. He was drunk and looked pissed off for some reason. I dared not...' said Arjun.

'What happened next?'

'He walked across the parking space to the lobby, and I saw him get into the elevator. I went back to my post.'

'And you were here all the time?'

'Yes, barring the few times I had to use the bathroom. They were urgent calls, you know. My stomach is not doing too well. With all these street food...'

Agni did not let him finish. He had no patience to lend his ear to the dietary hardships of immigrants in Kolkata. He asked, 'Is the post usually empty when you have to use the bathroom?'

'It is... during the nights, sir. I'm the only one on duty at that time,' Arjun looked uncomfortable as he realized the potential implications of a vacant security post at any time during the night.

'Where is the bathroom?' Agni looked around.

'It's on the other side of the parking area, sir.'

'Which means, while you are in the bathroom, someone with a key to the lock on the main gate can get inside and you won't notice.'

Arjun nodded in concurrence. Agni and Arya exchanged glances.

'How did you find Mayank Kapoor?'

'Around three o' clock, I was here in the security office, when I heard a loud noise in the backyard! I could hear glass shattering and a car alarm going off. I ran to the rear of the building. A few cars are parked these days in the backyard. This parking area is running out of space.' Arjun paused for a moment and then continued, 'And then, I saw him on the roof of one of the cars. The windshield of the car was shattered. I could tell he was dead. There was blood on the roof of the car. His neck was broken, turned oddly to a side.' Arjun shivered as he remembered the gory sight. 'For a few minutes, I couldn't react. I didn't know what I should do. I then walked up to the car. One of his arms hung over the edge. I checked for his pulse, just to be sure, with my eyes turned away from him. I couldn't bring myself to look at his face. He was dead. I started screaming. When I looked up, I saw many of the residents in their balconies. The sound had woken them up. Mr Pradip Samaddar was there too. Have you met him? He is the chairman of the cooperative and lives next door to Mayank sir's flat...'

'Yes, we've met him. What did you do next?'

'Mr Samaddar came down. He was followed by some of the other residents. The lights had come on inside most of the flats. Mr Samaddar informed the police. After a while, the police arrived.'

'What happened then?'

'The siren of the police car had woken up people in the neighbourhood. There were faces on the windows of the adjacent buildings. One of the cops stayed with Mayank sir's body. I picked up the master key and went up with the other one. We unlocked the door of his flat. We looked into every room. His flat was empty. The door to the bedroom balcony was open. We realized he had jumped from there. More cops turned up after some time. More people came down. Some of them started taking pictures on their phones—I couldn't believe my eyes! I thought that was rather insensitive. Don't you think so? People from the neighbouring apartments also started coming out. Word had got around and soon there were random people all over the place. The cops had a tough time managing the crowd.'

Arjun paused and took a sip from a glass of water on the table. They had been joined by the guard from the day shift. He introduced himself as Mohan.

Agni looked at the register. 'Looks like you maintain a log of people going into and out of the complex.'

'Yes, sir. Everyone needs to sign in and out.'

'Do you remember who visited Mayank Kapoor that day?' He picked up the register and started going through the logs.

'Sir was out in the morning. He returned in the afternoon with his friend.' Agni sensed a slight hesitation in Arjun's voice. 'Then he went out with her in the evening.'

'Do you know this friend?' Agni probed.

'Yes! She visited him a number of times in the last couple of months. Rituja Bose... you know, the famous actress.'

Chapter 40

Agni looked at Arya. His brows were wrinkled.

After a few minutes, he looked up from the register and said, 'On a number of days, I see big gaps in time between consecutive entries. It is very unlikely that none of the apartments here had any visitor for such lengths of time! Anything I'm missing here?'

There was hesitation in Arjun's voice as he replied, 'Well, some of the residents have *friends* who also have duplicate keys to the lock on the main gate. So, if any of them enters the premises when the post is empty for some reason, there will be no record.'

Agni threw his hands up in despair. The guards realized that they had already given out a lot more than they should have. They were not sure if their jobs were safe anymore, thanks to the detective.

'So, who were the *regular visitors* of Mayank Kapoor?'

'His heroines mostly... and then, some of his guy friends,' the guards replied, almost in chorus.

'You said Rituja Bose had been a regular for the last couple of months,' Agni looked into Arjun's eyes.

'Yes, she was. We know her.'

Agni picked up the register and handed it over to Arya.

'I want you to make a list of everyone who visited Mayank in the last three months. I want to find out who his regular visitors were.'

Agni turned to Arjun and asked, 'Do you remember seeing anyone get out of the elevator before you went to the rear of the building on hearing the crash and the alarm?'

'No one, sir. At least not when I was in the post. The last I had seen anyone use the elevator was Mayank sir going up,' Arjun confirmed.

'That would be all for now,' Agni finally let the two guards go.

When they came out of the complex, Agni turned towards Arya.

'If Mayank Kapoor was the last person to use the elevator that night before Mr Samaddar came down, the elevator car could not have been at the ground floor,' Agni said.

Arya's jaw dropped as the realization dawned on him.

Agni continued, 'Which means, someone had come down by that elevator before Mr Samaddar came down. Most probably, the murderer sneaked out when Mr Samaddar was in his bedroom balcony and Arjun had left his post to go to the backyard after hearing the crash.'

Chapter 41

◇◇◇◇◇◇◇◇◇◇

When Agni was ushered into the first-floor sitting area by one of Rituja's personal attendants, memories came flooding back to him and he could not shake off the uneasiness that had crept inside him the moment he had stepped into the same bungalow after more than a decade.

Rituja stepped out of her bedroom in a gown, her hair tied back neatly. It did not look like she had slept well.

'Good morning, Agni,' she said as she took a seat, pushing herself back on the sofa and crossing her legs. 'I'm afraid we'll have to keep this really short. I'm not too well.'

'This won't take too long, Ms Bose,' Agni said reassuringly.

An attendant placed a tall glass of orange juice on the table in front of Rituja.

'This is about Mayank,' Agni said.

Rituja took a sip of the juice. She did not speak, and her lips were pursed. It seemed she was struggling to hold back a deluge of emotions. Agni heard the birds outside and the general stirrings of the city waking up and going about its business on a cold winter morning.

When Rituja looked back at Agni, her eyes were moist.

'What about him?' she asked, a slight tremor in her voice.

'Where were you that night?' Agni finally broke the deafening silence.

Rituja tilted her head slightly and looked into Agni's eyes. There was a hint of smile at the corner of her lips.

145

'Am I a suspect, Agni? Do you *actually* think I could kill Mayank? Is that why you decided to pay me an early morning visit?'

'It's my job to explore all possibilities. He was seen last at Tipple with you. I was there myself,' Agni did not take his eyes off Rituja as he kept talking. 'And from the looks of it, your conversation with Mayank that night didn't seem to have ended on a happy note. I've been wondering if that conversation had anything to do with what happened later that night.'

Rituja threw her hands up, expressing her dismay at the suggestion.

'Look Agni, we were working together in a movie, in case you don't know. It is perfectly normal for artistes to have creative differences. What you saw inside Tipple was one of our usual arguments. Please don't read too deep into it, and try to relate it to the tragedy to make your job easy.'

She paused briefly and said, 'Were you in Tipple that night? Why didn't you walk over and join us? You could've heard everything we were *fighting about* and we would not be having this conversation now. Well, not that I mind having you back in my house.'

Agni did not respond. He said, 'Mayank looked very upset when he left Tipple. I know he went back to Galaxy from there. Where did *you* go from Tipple?'

Rituja lit a cigarette. She took a long drag and looked outside. She seemed to be contemplating her answer to Agni's question.

She let out a deep sigh. She then looked back at Agni, having made up her mind.

'Well, if you *have* to know, I spent the night with Rakesh Raheja in his bungalow near Narendrapur. He picked me up from Tipple.'

'Rakesh Raheja... you mean the producer?'

'Yes, *that* Rakesh. If you want to verify, you can speak to him. There is also the cook at his bungalow and the guards. They are of course sworn to secrecy. Rakesh doesn't like his wife to find out about the women he takes to his bungalow. But I hope Rakesh will speak the truth if he gets to know that his silence or denial would take me to the gallows!' Rituja smiled. 'By the way, I'm eyeing Rakesh's next project. Fingers crossed.' She made the sign with her fingers, suddenly looking like a child.

'Sounds like a pretty solid alibi, Ms Bose,' Agni smiled.

He looked at his watch and stood up.

'I really wish we could talk some more but I am already late,' Rituja sounded apologetic.

Agni looked at her with his eyes narrowed. Why did he have the feeling that Rituja knew much more than she was willing to divulge?

'I'm sure we'll have lots to talk about in days to come,' he said.

Chapter 42

Agni appraised himself in the mirror one more time. Fashion for him meant being in clothes that made him feel comfortable and confident. However, he was on his way to Rocky Chowdhury's workshop that morning, and did not want to be dismissed outright as a 'fashion disaster'. He paired his white shirt with a pair of faded blue jeans and put on his black blazer. That was conventional and comfortable, though in defiance of the rather rebellious designs that Rocky was famous for.

As he got into his car, Agni reflected on the progress he had made in the last couple of days.

The autopsy report for Mayank revealed that he had died around three in the morning. A combination of head injuries and internal blood loss had resulted in instant death. There had been severe injuries to the head, including multiple skull fractures, ruptures of brain structures and severe intra-cranial bleeding. There had also been severe injuries to other internal organs. Those included lung injuries, rib fractures and liver rupture.

Although Mayank's mobile phone was yet to be found, the activity details for his number were made available to the police by the service provider. An examination of call records revealed that, on the day of his demise, Mayank had spoken to and texted Rocky on several occasions. Agni found from the records that the two had been talking to each other several times every day over the last few months. In fact, Mayank texted Rocky around half past eleven on that fateful night after his return to his flat, an observation that prompted Agni's visit to the fashion designer that morning.

Another number that featured prominently in Mayank's call records belonged to Rituja. He had called and exchanged texts with her several times on that fateful day. Mayank was, of course, with Rituja in his flat that afternoon as the security guard testified. Later, Mayank was at Tipple with her in the evening— Agni was there himself. Mayank reached his flat alone at quarter past eleven, and the security guard heard him fall to his death around three o'clock.

In all probability, between quarter past eleven and three, someone entered the building with a duplicate key unnoticed, taking advantage of the security guard's absence from his post, took the elevator up to Mayank's flat, pushed Mayank off the edge of the bedroom balcony, and came down by the elevator when the security guard had rushed to the backyard on hearing the sound of Mayank's fall on the car and the car alarm.

Agni was convinced the mastermind behind the plan was someone who was no stranger to the apartment complex. The murderer, undoubtedly, was known to Mayank and had a duplicate key to the lock on the main gate. The murderer was also familiar with the security arrangements at Galaxy and the layout of the complex. That the murderer was familiar to Mayank was further corroborated by the fact that, there was no sign of a forced entry into Mayank's flat, or any indication of a scuffle inside. A thorough scrutiny of the visitors' book should throw up the names of those who had visited Mayank frequently over the last three months. Was Mayank's death related to the murders of Hiya and Lakhan? Agni did not know yet.

***

When Agni pressed the calling bell at the address he had, the door was opened by a woman with green streaks in her hair.

Her lips were distractingly glossy and her junk jewellery made jingling noises at the slightest movement of her hands or neck. She put a hand on her unbelievably narrow waist and fixed her large kohl-rimmed eyes on Agni.

'Yes?'

'I've got an appointment with Mr Chowdhury at eleven,' Agni looked at his watch. He was around ten minutes early. 'I am ACP Agni Mitra from Kolkata Police,' he added.

'Please be seated,' the woman gestured to a few colourful chairs in the reception area. 'I'll let him know,' the 'him' was accompanied by a slight backward tilt of her oval head in the direction of an adjoining room which had its door closed.

She set off for the room, and then stopped, turning around to face Agni.

'Oh, by the way, don't *ever* call him *Mr Chowdhury*. He hates that! He's Rocky—*just* Rocky—for everyone,' she laughed, revealing stained teeth, probably from heavy smoking if not from more damaging addictions, and walked away.

A few minutes passed before Rocky stepped out of one of the adjoining rooms and approached Agni. Agni noticed the characteristic swing of his hips even as his upper body and arms remained remarkably still as he walked.

He wore a purple t-shirt that was a second skin and his white jeans clung to his hips and slender legs. He ran his fingers through his messy locks and stretched out a very cold and soft hand.

Rocky gestured at Agni to follow him as he started walking back towards the room he had appeared from. On his way, he hollered at the girl at the reception, 'I'll be busy for the next half an hour. No calls and no guests, please. And send in some green tea for us, sweetheart.'

Agni realized his time would be up in half an hour, and that Rocky did not believe in checking for one's preference when it came to beverages.

Agni peered into a room to his right which had its door ajar, and saw a few mannequins in various stages of undress, studio lights, heaps of clothes, workbenches and walls decorated with garish paintings. Agni could see another woman inside the room, working on a dress.

Rocky pointed a slender finger towards the room and said, 'Those are from my upcoming Spring-Summer collection, still work-in-progress. I'm planning a seriously big launch this year,' without bothering to stop or to look at Agni.

Rocky pushed open the door to his office and the first thing that struck Agni was the chill inside the room. The air conditioner was on in full blast, which Agni found rather unusual considering the time of the year.

'Phew, never seen a warmer winter, have you?' Rocky turned towards Agni as he fanned himself animatedly with his hands.

Agni buttoned up his blazer and smiled. The chill was getting to his bones.

There was a large desk strewn with sketches, crayons, felt pens and markers. There was an ash-tray overflowing with cigarette stubs. Rocky walked around the desk and sat down on a high back chair, the leather making fart noises as he landed on it. He gestured toward a similar chair on the other side of the desk for Agni.

The walls were whitewashed and had framed pictures, mostly in black and white, all over. Agni looked around the room. He could see Mayank Kapoor in most of the pictures around him.

'Cute boy, wasn't he?' Rocky asked, noticing Agni.

'Oh yes, a very good-looking man,' Agni finally heard something he could agree with. 'Looks like you worked a lot with him!' Agni commented.

'I did,' Rocky lit a cigarette and offered Agni one, which he politely refused. 'Mayank walked the ramp for me on many occasions.' Rocky pointed at one of the pictures with his cigarette. 'See that one? That was about a week back. He was my showstopper.'

He shook his head and said, 'It'd be hard to find another Mayank. He could carry off anything! What a darling!'

He then took a long drag of the cigarette, his eyes closed.

When he opened his eyes, they were moist.

'What a way to go!' Rocky sighed, blowing out a lot of smoke through his nostrils.

'Indeed,' Agni muttered. He had not foreseen the emotional turn the conversation had taken.

'You know, ACP, he was so full of life! His energy was infectious,' Rocky was still reclined in his chair, his eyes closed, restlessly taking long drags of the cigarette and blowing through his nose. He pulled his unruly locks off his face with both his hands. 'We've spent days and nights here, right in this workshop, discussing fashion, movies, music... and love! I've lost a great friend, ACP. All I have now are these pictures...'

'I understand you were very close to him. And I believe the two of you spoke a number of times on that fateful day.'

'Yes, we did. I was designing his clothes for his new movie with Rituja. Actually, we were very busy in the days before his... his...' Rocky stopped; his voice choked.

'What do *you* think might have driven Mayank to...'

Rocky did not let Agni finish. In fact, it seemed he did not want him to finish. He suddenly thumped on the desk, almost in anticipation of what Agni was about to say, dislodging in the process a few sheets of paper that drifted to the floor. 'Don't... please don't... say that word!'

Agni was overwhelmed by Rocky's grief for the man he had loved with all his heart and who had probably never been his, and he was reminded all over again of the myriad hues of love and its all-consuming prowess.

Chapter 43

The girl Agni had met outside in the reception area stepped into the room with a tray carrying two cups of green tea and a plate with cookies. She looked sympathetically at Rocky and scornfully at Agni, in turns. She hurriedly placed the tray on the desk and left, after yet another reproachful glance at Agni, who had clearly earned her wrath for having caused visible distress to the boss.

Rocky removed his glasses. The veins in his eyes were red. He went on, 'Mayank could never have done that to himself! Never!' Rocky's thin, almost tinny voice reverberated in the closed room. His locks were all over his face now, the eyes barely visible.

'If I may ask, what makes you so confident?' Agni bent forward.

'You don't see, do you? He was *happy!* He was very happy all through that day. We were on the phone so many times! I kept asking him, but he wouldn't tell me. He was being such a tease! I was dying to know. He was with Rituja in the afternoon. They went out for a drink. Tipple... I think that's where they went that evening. And then, that text from him...' Rocky lamented.

'He texted you at half past eleven, fifteen minutes after he reached home that night,' Agni said.

'Yes,' Rocky lit another cigarette and took a long drag noisily. He closed his eyes and stroked his stubble. The only sounds in the room were those of his frequent drags on the cigarette and the hum of the air-conditioner.

'What was the message about, if I may ask?' Agni sounded impatient.

153

Rocky picked up his phone from the desk and scrolled through the messages in his inbox till he found Mayank's last message to him. With his eyes fixed on the phone screen, Rocky almost whispered, 'He said that he had good news for me... that he would tell me when we met the next morning... said he was going to bed... poor baby... never got to see the new day he had been waiting for...' Rocky sniffled.

'I don't think I saw you at Galaxy the next day,' Agni immediately wondered if it was alright to bring up that reference. Rocky did not reprimand him this time, to Agni's relief.

'I didn't go. I wanted to live with my memories of the last time we had met. He sat right where you are sitting now. We went through some of the designs for his new movie. That was a day before the... the...'

Agni looked at his watch and stood up. It was well past the half hour that had been originally stipulated for him.

He stretched out his hand. When Rocky took his hand in his, Agni said, 'Rocky, thanks for your time! And I sincerely hope that you'll find the strength to get over your loss.'

As he walked out of the room, Agni looked back. Rocky was still in his chair, which was now turned in the direction of the picture of Mayank's last ramp-walk. Agni could see tears streaming down his chubby cheeks.

Rocky was madly in love with Mayank, the man who had fallen in love with Hiya and had probably not managed to erase her memories or the grief of her betrayal till the last day of his life.

Unrequited love was always a dangerous motivation.

Chapter 44

Agni's car crunched on the gravel as he drove into the portico of the Chauhans' lavish bungalow. He turned the ignition off and stepped out, where he was greeted by a valet, who promptly offered to drive his car to the garage.

An immaculately dressed woman was waiting for him at the top of the three stairs that led up to the spacious sitting area. The watchman at the main gate had called her to announce Agni's arrival.

'Hi, I'm Devina. Please do have a seat, ACP Mitra. Sir would be here right away. Is there anything I can bring for you – tea, coffee?' Devina rattled off, almost mechanically, plastic smile intact all through her routine welcome address.

'A black coffee please, no sugar,' Agni requested, as he lowered himself into a cane chair with fluffy cushions. As he waited for Manav Chauhan, his eyes went to the impeccably maintained lawns and he soaked in the soothing tranquillity of the surroundings.

The day's newspapers were strewn on a cane table. The *Economic Journal* carried an interview with Manav on the front page. The interview was about the impact of inflation on the purchasing habits of the Indian middle class and what that meant for Manav's business. Agni looked at the picture that accompanied the interview. It showed Manav smiling broadly at the camera in a t-shirt. The background looked familiar. It was the *Sher-e-Punjab* restaurant off the Kolkata-Mumbai Highway. The tricolour was prominently displayed. There was a board near the top of the entrance that read 'Happy Independence Day 2022'. Agni felt that Manav's jovial countenance did not go too well with the not-so-upbeat tone of the interview.

'Precisely what happens when it is your fiancée who chooses the picture to go with your interview. They find you charming in every damn picture, don't they? I hate my silly grin!' said Manav, as he walked in and could gauge Agni's reaction to the picture accompanying the newspaper article. Agni looked up from the newspaper and saw Manav standing right in front of him, smiling, a hand stretched out.

Agni shook his hand and smiled back.

'You would know better, Mr Chauhan,' he said, suddenly realizing Manav had just confirmed the rumours about his impending second marriage.

'The journalist called up at the last minute for a picture,' continued Manav as he took a chair right opposite Agni, 'I was in the shower and Neha mailed her the first picture she found in my laptop. From a long drive she and I had gone to! Lesson learnt – never ever let your fiancée play with your laptop when you are not around!' Both men laughed aloud.

There went the second confirmation! It was Neha, indeed, who was going to be the next Mrs Chauhan.

'Well, if nothing else, the picture will probably bring some cheer to the despondent market,' Agni remarked as he folded the newspaper neatly and laid it down on the table. They laughed again.

One of the Chauhans' servants had, in the meantime, served coffee and some cookies on a plate. Agni picked up his cup and took a sip.

Manav looked at him and asked, 'It's always a pleasure talking to you, ACP Mitra. But I have a feeling this is not really a social visit, is it?'

Agni smiled, 'Looks like my social skills have not made a healthy impression on you!' He paused briefly and then said, 'Well, you are right, actually. I'm here on business. I wanted to talk to you about Mayank Kapoor.'

'That was absolutely shocking!' Manav shook his head. There was a faraway look in his eyes as he said, 'We used to be fast friends.'

'So I heard,' said Agni.

'We gave him the first modelling break when he came down to Kolkata from Patna. He kept working with us ever since. In between, a number of other prestigious brands signed him up. He started acting in TV serials. I heard he also bagged a movie deal sometime back.'

'Were you in touch with him lately?'

'Well, he got busy with his career. I was, of course, holed up in the hospital for most of the past few months. To be honest, we didn't really get to see a lot of each other in the recent past.'

'Didn't he visit you at the hospital?'

Manav thought for a few seconds and then said, 'I did hear from Neha that he had come down to see me the day after the accident. But I was unconscious at that time, and we couldn't meet.'

'I do understand,' Agni nodded. He took his time before he asked the next question.

'Is it true that there was an altercation between the two of you in a movie set some time back? I believe Hiya was working in that movie.' He reclined in his chair, and fixed his eyes on Manav, who looked back at Agni without flinching.

'Well, yes! Where did you hear about that?' Manav questioned Agni back without answering. Agni sensed a slight resentment in Manav's voice.

'I had the opportunity to speak to Mayank a few days before his death. Through a common friend, you know...'

Manav shook his head and blew through his mouth. He looked away; his eyes narrowed. 'Mayank and his *friends*!' he exclaimed. 'You know what? He fell into bad company when he started working in the serials. He lost control on the drinking. I heard he had started doing drugs too. He was a changed man.'

Manav paused briefly and then said, 'I am not the kind that washes dirty linen in public. I didn't want to discuss what I still feel was a family scandal. But now that you already know it, I might as well tell you. Yes, there was some friction between Mayank and me over Hiya. It was rather unexpected, if you ask me. I thought the guy was out of his mind!'

'But that incident probably scarred your friendship for good!'

Manav had that faraway look on his face again. 'It probably did, when I come to think of it. I'm sure Mayank regretted his actions too, but he never managed to bring himself to coming up to me and talking. It does take a lot of courage to do that, doesn't it?' He paused and took a sip of the coffee, looking distraught. He then continued, 'And I kept thinking that I'd eventually extend the olive branch myself. But then, sometimes it gets too late. That's what life teaches us! Mayank must've died a troubled soul!'

'Yes, Mr Chauhan. He did regret the incident. When I spoke to him, he was upset over the uncertainty around the future of his relationship with you.'

When Agni looked at Manav, he spotted the glint of tear at the corner of an eye. He allowed Manav to regain his composure and then asked him, 'How did you get to know about his death, Mr Chauhan?'

'I was at Salt Lake that night at the inauguration of the Awasthis' new restaurant in my mall there. The event was widely covered by the media. I came to know about Mayank's death like everyone else, through the internet and the television and the newspapers the next morning. And that's what makes it all so difficult! It was not meant to be like this, at all! Considering how close we were...' Agni could sense Manav's pain.

For a few minutes, no word passed between the two men. The silence was broken by the clatter of heels.

Devina looked almost apologetically at Agni and turned towards Manav.

'Sir, Mr Suri has arrived. You have an appointment.'

Agni did not let her finish and stood up. He was interested in Manav's version of the account he had heard earlier from Mayank. He had already got that story validated.

'Thanks for your time, Mr Chauhan. I understand your feelings,' Agni paused briefly and said, 'Happens with all of us. Sometimes it does get too late, and everything changes before we know.'

Chapter 45

Agni looked at the sluggish traffic on the road below, cradling a glass of whiskey, his mind in turmoil. As he drained the glass, his eyes closed, images from the last few months kept flashing through his mind. He remembered his interrogation of the three convicts. He remembered his rendezvous with Anamika inside Panache and everything she had said about Neha Awasthi. He remembered what Arya had found out about the decline in Deepak Awasthi's fortunes. He recalled his meetings with Rituja and the report about her very public spat with Hiya. His mind drifted to the private booth inside The Nook, where he had met Mayank for the first time, intoxicated and hurt. He remembered Manav's parents regretting their son's decision to marry Hiya and the 'misfortune that the girl had brought on the family'. He remembered the accounts of Hiya's secretary and her director about the emotional turmoil she had been going through in the days leading up to her marriage, and about her reckless affair with Mayank, which had taken everyone by surprise. The image of Lakhan lying dead in a pool of blood next to a gutter inside a Tiljala slum flashed before his eyes. He remembered the unlikely affluence he had noticed inside Lakhan's rented house and the hefty sums of money that had been deposited in his bank account from time to time since Hiya's murder. He remembered seeing Mayank walk out of Tipple and Rituja try to placate him on the night of his murder. What was the good news he wanted to share with Rocky the next morning? The image of Mayank lying dead on the roof of a car came next. In his mind, Agni found himself back in Mayank's flat, wandering from room to room. He saw Rocky, shedding silent tears as he looked at the pictures of Mayank inside his dark, cold office.

Mayank – so very different in his pictures from his real brooding self.

Those pictures – in Rocky's workshop, inside Mayank's own flat.

And then suddenly, something clicked inside Agni's mind. Agni was jerked to complete alertness, and he sat up straight under the forceful impact of his sudden realization of a fantastic possibility. In his excitement, Agni jumped off his deck chair. He started pacing up and down his room, talking to himself.

He had to meet Rituja.

But, before that, he had to call Neha Awasthi.

Chapter 46

A pall of silence descended inside the room when Rituja finished speaking.

Agni leaned back and let out a deep sigh. The fantastic revelation Rituja had laid bare before Agni a while back had not sunk in fully yet. His eyes were fixed on the particles of dust swimming in the cone of light that seeped in through the glass window. The black coffee on the table in front of him had gone cold long back.

Rituja reclined in her couch and lit yet another cigarette, coughing mildly. She passed her fingers through her dishevelled hair. Her eyes were fixed on the wall ahead, and they had a sheen of tears. Free from make-up, her face looked puffy and the lines on it were prominent. Rituja looked aged and weary.

When Agni looked back at her, he saw a woman living in self-denial, trying desperately to hold on to the last vestiges of the stardom that had abandoned her years back. She was the reason why Agni would rush to the theatres several years back. She was the one who gave him sleepless nights of untold pain and despair in his early years in the force. Destiny had brought them together after a decade.

Agni stood up and said, 'I don't have the words to thank you, Ms Bose...'

'Ritu,' she interrupted.

'By the way, why did you let me in on your secret about Mayank? When we spoke the last time, you tried to hold on to it, giving me a very different and inaccurate impression about what the two of you had been talking about inside Tipple that night!'

'I always owed you one, Agni. I realized it late. But what matters is that I did realize, after all. I'll be happy if this piece of information helps you in any way.' Rituja smiled warmly at Agni and continued, 'You know what? I don't know what you made of my relationship with Mayank from what you saw, but I've always been very protective about him. Almost in a maternal way. Behind that mask of a tough exterior, he was weak and vulnerable. I made a promise to Mayank and I am proud I kept my word. I knew if word got out, the industry might not have been kind to him. I didn't want him to join the league of actors whose careers have been ruined. But, he's no more and it doesn't matter anymore,' Rituja sniffled, and her voice choked. 'I want, as much as you do, to get to the bottom of this, and find out who did this to him. And one more thing, Agni.'

Rituja stood up and walked towards Agni.

Standing at an arm's length, she ruffled his hair, leaving him stunned.

She looked into his eyes and said, 'I... I am sorry for everything. I know it's too late. Many years have passed. But I have to say this. You didn't deserve what you went through ten years back. I was a stupid, arrogant girl who thought that the world was at her feet and would stay there forever. What I didn't realize was that time is no one's best friend!' Her tears spilled over.

Agni smiled. Sometimes, the deepest of wounds need the simplest of words to heal.

'Stay well, Ritu.' He finally called her by her name, the way she always wanted him to. It took him ten years to bring himself to do that.

Agni turned around and headed out. He had to pick up Arya and head for the Sher-e-Punjab restaurant on the Kolkata-Mumbai highway.

Chapter 47

Agni woke up with a start as the mobile phone buzzed under his pillow.

He picked up the phone. It was Rocky.

His eyes went to the wall clock in front of him. It was close to ten in the morning. He had overslept. The drive to Sher-e-Punjab dhaba and back the day before with Arya was strenuous. Arya and he were then up till late, validating his theories with the information they had gathered at the restaurant.

'Good morning, Agni,' Rocky's voice sounded heavier than usual.

'Good morning, Rocky. Are you alright?'

Rocky did not reply.

'Agni, can you please come over?'

'To your workshop?'

'Yes... we *have* to meet!' Rocky almost pleaded with him.

'What's going on, Rocky?' Agni was already out of bed, heading towards the toilet.

'There's something I want you to know. Preeti came down to my workshop this morning. She is a friend. She works for a travel agency.'

It seemed to Agni that, Rocky was in deep emotional stress for some reason. He sounded disoriented on the phone as he kept on talking.

Chapter 48

The conical sabres of light outside Vibe, the auditorium inside the Town Centre Mall, the Chauhans' multi-storeyed property in Salt Lake, were visible from miles away. They moved in rhythm with the loud music, criss-crossing each other, and lighting up the night sky. There was a fashion show on at Vibe that evening to launch Rocky's new Spring-Summer collection.

The Town Centre Mall in Salt Lake had emerged as the hottest shopping destination in Kolkata in just a few months. The Awasthis had opened a restaurant in the mall sometime back – the same restaurant that was inaugurated by Manav on the night of Mayank's murder.

Rocky had invited Agni to the event when they had met briefly in the morning. 'We're using pre-recorded digital videos as backdrop for the ramp for the first time ever in Kolkata...you'll get to see the vibrant hues of spring and feel the romance in the air as my models sashay down the ramp!' Rocky had proudly announced.

As Agni and Arya walked into Vibe, they could barely hear each other's voice above the music. Some of the top models of the city were on the ramp in the dresses designed by Rocky. A couple of designs seemed familiar to Agni. He had seen them when he visited Rocky in his workshop.

Agni spotted a galaxy of celebrities in the front row, Manav Chauhan included. He sat next to Neha. Agni also saw Deepak Awasthi, who turned his face away when their eyes met. The media presence was remarkable, everyone jostling for the best view. Agni noticed logos of some of the most popular television channels and media houses.

As Agni and Arya found their seats, Agni pulled out his phone and spoke into it.

For the next several minutes, Agni's eyes darted between the ramp and the front row decorated with Rocky's celebrity guests. The high-octane music which made conversation impossible was interrupted only by the frequent collective gasps and applause from the audience as the models walked in one awe-inspiring design after another, the grandeur of all of it completely lost on Agni.

Rocky had just finished his bow before the ecstatic audience with all his models and walked back up the ramp, when Agni saw Manav pull out his phone.

He seemed to be reading something. He then looked around. After a few seconds, he left his seat and headed for one of the exits.

Chapter 49

Stepping into the roof-top parking lot of the Town Centre Mall, Manav looked around. It was late in the evening, closer to night in fact, and the roof was desolate. The icy cold wind licked his face. He buttoned up his jacket and looked around one more time as he took a couple of tentative steps. A few cars were scattered around. Not a soul was in sight anywhere. Not even the security staff who, Manav thought, should have been there. He made a mental note. He would have to take this up with the agency.

The light sabres from Vibe moved in circles, piercing through the darkness of the night. The beats of the loud music reached his ears. He fished out his phone from a pocket and read the text from the unknown number one more time.

Need to discuss some matters. Meet me on the roof of the mall right now, alone.

If this was someone's idea of a joke, it was not funny. For a moment, Manav regretted having paid heed to the message. He also wondered if he should have informed someone from the security or got one of the guards to accompany him, irrespective of what the sender of the message had instructed.

Before Manav could do anything more than just turn around in the direction of the lift lobby, a figure pounced on him from the shadows and sent him crashing against the boundary wall of the roof before he could react.

Manav tried to get up, but his assailant was pressing a knee down on his back. From the corner of his eye, Manav looked at the man, as he grabbed Manav by the hair and threw his face down on the cement floor of the roof. Even in the split second that he was allowed, Manav could recognize Rocky.

'Rocky? Is that you? What the fuck do you think you are doing?' Manav was shocked.

Paying no heed, Rocky tightened his hold on Manav's hair. He then jerked Manav's head upward and then down, once again, onto the cement floor of the roof with a violent smack. There were shock waves that spread through Manav's skull, almost jarring the roots of his clenched teeth. Everything slowed down around Manav, as he felt blood streaming past his eyes. His arms and legs suddenly felt numb when he tried once again to get up on his knees.

'Rocky, why are you...' Manav barely managed to speak as another pile-driving punch landed on his jaw. Manav tried to raise his head, but he felt searing pain in his head, and bile rising up his throat. He felt wobbly and disoriented.

Rocky grabbed Manav by the hair and raised his head from the floor. Manav had lost the strength to resist. Rocky brought his face close to Manav's ears and screamed like a man possessed, 'I've suffered enough, Manav Chauhan! Enough! It's your turn now!'

He started dragging Manav along the roof towards the edge, when suddenly the silence of the night was shattered by the sound of a gunshot in the air.

Rocky was momentarily distracted, and he turned around.

Agni stood a few feet away, his gun firmly trained on Rocky.

'Enough, Rocky! No one dies tonight! This madness has to stop!'

Chapter 50

Rocky could hear more footsteps on the stairs.

Without flinching from his position, his gun still firmly trained between Rocky's eyes, Agni looked from the corner of his eye at the figure running past him in the direction of Rocky. It was Arya.

'Rocky, I won't say this again!' Agni thundered. 'Let go of Mr Chauhan!'

With his eyes fixed on Agni, Rocky kept holding on to Manav. He was immediately intercepted by Arya, who struggled to pull him away. Like a vengeful beast forced to let go of its prey, Rocky grunted in fury, trying to set himself free from Arya's hold. Manav wobbled to his feet and limped to a safe distance away from Rocky. His lips were split and blood from the crack in his forehead coursed past his eyes down his jaw.

Agni could see the blind rage still simmering in Rocky's eyes, his hands tainted with Manav's blood. With his eyes fixed on Agni, Rocky finally lowered himself on his knees on the roof. Agni lowered his gun, still aiming at Rocky.

Rocky gulped hard and inched closer to Agni on his knees.

'Shoot me, ACP... shoot me please!' He pleaded. His voice sounded eerie.

'Rocky, stop playing games with me! You are going to land up in jail on charges of assault.'

'I beg of you,' Rocky was now less than a foot away. Rocky was provoking him, but Agni was not going to bite the bait.

Standing behind Rocky, Arya pulled out his gun and trained it at the back of Rocky's skull.

A menacing grimace was frozen on Rocky's face. The rage in his eyes was slowly giving way to despair, as tears started rolling down his cheeks. With his hands folded, Rocky moved still closer.

He was about six inches away from Agni now.

'Agni, I failed you. And I'm sorry... I'm so sorry!' With his head bowed, Rocky started beating the floor of the roof. 'I know... I know we talked about this in the morning. But... but... I love him... I love Mayank... and I will... till my last breath. You know that, don't you?' He said in between bouts of crying. He rubbed his face with his hands, smearing it red with Manav's blood making it look ghoulish. He turned his face to a side, now howling uncontrollably, casting a spiteful glance at Manav.

Agni inched closer with his gun in anticipation. Arya released the lock of his.

'Don't get ideas, Rocky! And don't you force me to pull the trigger!' Agni said in a cold voice.

Manav tottered close to Rocky.

'You are in love with Mayank? You are? And... and... is that why you finished off the woman *he* was in love with?' Manav spoke through his clenched teeth. 'That woman was *my wife,* you scumbag!'

'Mr Chauhan, get a grip on yourself!' Agni raised his voice.

'And what about Mayank? What made you kill your *darling,* you fucking monster! Your sweet little revenge, was it? Because he didn't love you back and went after my wife?' Manav screamed maniacally, ignoring Agni's warning. 'Because he loved Hiya, and not you? And... and why me now? You are on a fucking mission to finish off everyone Mayank was close to, aren't you, you jealous shithead?' Manav got on his knees and reached for Rocky's neck.

Agni's gun moved a few degrees, as Manav turned his head towards Agni, his jaw dropping.

'ACP Mitra, what do you think you are...' A light beam from several feet below swam across Manav's unbelieving face.

The wind began to rise, whistling across the roof.

'Mr Chauhan, let me tell you this. Mayank never had any genuine interest in Hiya. *He was gay.*'

Chapter 51

'Are you out of your mind? He had an affair with my fiancée, for god's sake! Half the world knows that!' Manav stood up, grimacing immediately with the acute pain he felt. 'And why the fuck do you have that gun trained on me?'

'Because I don't want you to act smart while I explain to you why I'm *not* out of my mind,' Agni's voice sounded menacingly calm. 'Do you know that Mayank was in Tipple with Rituja the night he was murdered? You probably do. What you don't know is that I too was in Tipple that night. I saw the two of them. Having a good laugh. Enjoying their drinks. And then, something happened. I saw Mayank get agitated, restless. Rituja tried to explain something to him. Mayank left the club, even as Rituja tried to hold him back.'

'Good to know, ACP. But what has this got to do with your fantastic theory? And it still doesn't explain why I have a gun aimed at my fucking skull!'

'Don't you want to know what the two of them were talking about that night?'

'I don't think I care,' Manav shrugged.

'Of course you do! As much as I did, Mr Chauhan. So, I asked Rituja.' Agni moved closer to Manav. 'And this is what she told me. Mayank had decided to leave Kolkata. He had decided to throw away his modelling opportunities, to end his budding career in the movies.'

Rocky let out a heart-wrenching wail, his head turned skywards, otherwise motionless on his knees on the floor.

'Because his lover had promised to take him to London. He had been dreaming through the eyes of that man. Dreaming of a life together. A life of happiness, of peace, of security. Free from the stigma. Where people wouldn't think there was something wrong with him if he held the hand of the man he loved. His career, his fame, the flashlights, his fans – everything and everyone paled near the glow of that dream. Rituja was trying to make him see sense, pleading with him to be realistic. She has seen more of the world than Mayank had. She has trusted people and has been let down, again and again. Life has taught her not to surrender completely to dreams. One often ends up paying a heavy price.'

Agni tilted his head in the direction of Rocky, without taking his eyes off Manav. 'When I spoke to this man here, he told me the same thing. All through that day, Mayank was happy. The man with a battered soul was actually very happy that day! He texted Rocky that night, saying he had good news that he would share with Rocky when they met the next day.

'When I spoke to Rocky this morning, he confided in me. He said he was madly in love with Mayank, but he had realized that Mayank was someone else's. Mayank had told him that, he would soon be gone forever with the man he loved. And that broke Rocky's heart. But you know what, Mr Chauhan? When you love someone, you are happy when that person is happy, even if you are not part of that happiness. Rocky would never kill Mayank for his *sweet little revenge*. From whatever I know about Rocky, he can't fake his tears.'

Agni paused briefly and then continued. 'But Mayank never disclosed even to his closest friends who his lover was. He would say he was waiting for the right time. It's sad that he never found the right time, poor soul!'

Rocky kept sobbing, his tears forming rivulets down his face smeared with Manav's blood.

Manav staggered towards Agni.

'ACP, you probably haven't noticed but that man beat me to pulp a while back. I'm bleeding... and I'm not sure if it's only me, or you guys are feeling it too, it's awfully cold up here. I still don't know why on earth I'm being forced at gunpoint to listen to Mayank's love story!'

'Mr Chauhan, I'm going to tell you where exactly you come in! This morning in Rocky's workshop, I met Preeti who provided me with the evidence that my theory needed. '

'Now, who's Preeti?' Manav cut in.

Agni looked straight into Manav's eyes. 'She works for a travel agency and is a close friend of Rocky. She handles his travels across the country and abroad. Rocky had introduced her to Mayank. Mayank wanted to plan for a travel in confidence, and he needed to work with someone he could trust with his secret. She made the travel plan exactly as Mayank had wanted, and called him up the day before his murder. But Mayank did not live to collect the tickets and travel documents from her, and to make that trip with his partner. Preeti could not make up her mind for a few days whether she should come forward and share the details of Mayank's travel plan with anyone. After all, Mayank had wanted her to keep the plan a secret. And then, she realized that the details of the travel plan could provide a breakthrough in the police investigation. This morning, Preeti decided to talk to Rocky, and Rocky called me over. We pored over the travel documents she had brought along.

'Mayank and his lover had planned to take separate flights from Kolkata that landed in Mumbai in the space of a few hours. Mayank had planned to take the earlier flight. He was supposed to wait in Mumbai for his lover. The two of them were then supposed to board a late flight from Mumbai to London, together. Quite a plan, wasn't it?'

'I'm still waiting to hear where I come in, ACP,' Manav tried to force a smile.

'This is exactly where you come in, Mr Chauhan. The other name that's all over those travel documents – is yours! *Because the man who was in a relationship with Mayank is none other than you!*'

Chapter 52

Keeping his gun firmly trained on Manav, Arya looked sideways at Agni and asked, 'You never told me when this struck you as a possibility. I hate it when you keep secrets from me!'

'And I hate it when you sound like a bitter spouse, Arya!' Agni smiled. 'I'm sure Mr Chauhan has the same question, though he won't admit. I won't keep you guessing,' Agni turned towards Manav and continued.

'When Rituja told me that Mayank was gay, I was baffled, as I knew about his affair with your fiancée in the days before your wedding. Rituja told me she had been baffled herself when she had come to know about the affair. When she asked Mayank, he said that he was *putting on an act for a reason!* She was privy to Mayank's secret, but like a true friend, played along till the last day of Mayank's life.

This revelation got me thinking. What could Mayank's *reason* be? I realized that, the inevitable outcome of the staged affair and then the very public spat between Mayank and you was your breaking off the engagement. Something you had done earlier with Neha as well. There was an unmistakable behavioural pattern that repeated itself. That of the reluctant groom!'

'This is rubbish!' Manav almost screamed but sounded feeble in his defence.

'Mr Chauhan, my hypothesis gained further credence with another faux pas of yours.'

Manav's eyebrows were wrinkled.

'Let me play back to you these priceless words you said the other day— *never ever let your fiancée play with your laptop when you are not around.* You were right. Someone may end up using pictures that have stories to tell,' Agni's voice was steel cold. 'An otherwise innocent picture from a long drive, for instance.'

Manav's eyes were dilated. His lips trembled, but words failed him.

'You, Mr Chauhan, in a t-shirt. Smiling cheerfully at the camera. The Sher-e-Punjab restaurant off the Kolkata-Mumbai highway behind you, with the Tricolour prominently displayed. A board near the top of the entrance with the words "Happy Independence Day 2022"!' Agni paused briefly and then continued, 'It took me a while to figure out why that picture made me uneasy through an entire day. And then I remembered! I remembered later that night, that I had seen a similar picture on the wall in Mayank's bedroom. Mayank – in a t-shirt, smiling at the camera, Independence Day decorations at the entrance of the Sher-e-Punjab restaurant in the background. Same year. Same place.'

There was potent silence on the roof. The only sounds were those of the wind whispering ominously and the beats of music from the after-party down below. The chill was beginning to get to the bones of the men brought together by destiny at that vantage point towering over the city.

'I didn't get your point, ACP. What are you trying to prove? I told you I was there with Neha! Are you suggesting that Mayank and I couldn't have been in the same restaurant on the same day, ever? Even by chance? Oh, come on!' Manav retorted in defiance, but the effort showed.

'Sure, you could be! No doubt about that, Mr Chauhan. However, we have a different problem here. Those pictures were from the month of August. *You had broken up with Neha Awasthi well before that and the two of you had not even been in touch during that time, forget about going on a long drive on the highway!'*

Agni's words seemed to have sucked the air off Manav's chest. He gasped for breath.

'When I called Neha that night, she confirmed that she had not spent the Independence Day holiday this year with you. Contrary to what you had told me that morning. And just a minute ago, for that matter. That morning, when I visited you, I didn't ask you anything about that picture. It was you who volunteered that piece of false information, Mr Chauhan. Why did you lie to me?'

Manav flicked his tongue over his parched lips once again.

'Looks like you don't have an answer. Let me try. With that lie, you tried to hide something. That was nothing but classic behaviour of the guilty! Unsolicited explanation for something you subconsciously knew could land you in trouble. That picture *did* land you in trouble, Mr Chauhan. I drove down to the Sher-e-Punjab restaurant yesterday with Arya, and showed them the pictures – the one on Mayank's wall and yours on the newspaper. Everyone in the restaurant still remembers Mayank Kapoor dropping in on Independence Day. Many of the waiters had taken selfies with the hero of their favourite television serials! Some of them showed me the pictures. All of them said Mayank had come with a friend. They recognized you readily when they saw your picture. It's not the picture, Mr Chauhan, or your outing with Mayank, for that matter, but it's your unnecessary lie about that outing that strengthened my theory.

'You know what the irony is? Mayank displayed his memory of that long drive on his bedroom wall. You chose to hide your memory in a folder in your laptop. Just like everything else you've been hiding all these years. But, our lies always catch up with us.'

'Just as I thought! Just as I thought all these months,' Rocky turned around and scowled at Manav, 'From the way Mayank went on and on about you! I had a gut feeling... and I asked him many times. He kept denying... saying he would tell me at the right time. Thank god that good sense dawned on Preeti and she finally decided to see me this morning!'

Chapter 53

'ACP, I won't let you get away with this! You've no right to harass me with ridiculous figments of your overworked imagination!' Manav tried to sound authoritative, but his laboured breathing gave him away.

Rocky turned towards Agni and continued, 'We talked about this in the morning. You seemed to suggest that his lover might have done him in. I could not concentrate on the show. I saw the bastard sitting there in the front row, all smug and haughty, and I couldn't hold myself back anymore, ACP. I'm so sorry I failed you, asking him to meet me on the roof without telling you and beating the crap out of him just as he deserves! But I'm so sorry, ACP...' Rocky looked genuinely apologetic.

Manav pointed a finger at Rocky and hissed through his teeth, looking at Agni, 'What did he just say? Are you guys now trying to implicate me in Mayank's murder?'

'You heard him right, Mr Chauhan. Both of us know how Mayank fell to his death. *You pushed him off his bedroom balcony.*' Agni revealed.

Chapter 54

'What a fantastic idea! ACP, why don't you quit your job and start writing fiction?' Manav tried to force a laughter that sounded hopelessly fake. 'And while you gratify yourself with these ridiculous theories, may I ask you what could possibly be the motive for my murdering my *lover*, as you'd had me believe a few minutes back?'

'Motive, opportunity, means. You had everything, and I'll not leave anything out tonight. But let me start with a very simple question. Mr Chauhan, you've been living a double life for years now. You've been almost neurotically secretive about your steady relationship with Mayank. What are you afraid of?'

Manav kept looking at Agni with dead eyes, trying to force a dry smile. Agni suddenly felt sorry for the man standing battered and bruised in front of him, having taken the blows not just on his body, but also on his soul.

'Are you afraid of your overtly conservative family with its archaic values "disowning" you? And the impact such an "eviction" would potentially have on your flourishing career, on how the homophobic society would start looking at you? What are you afraid of, Mr Chauhan? Why this desperate need to pass off as *another* man with a wife and children when your heart is clearly not in it?' Agni screamed. 'You fail every time, but don't give up trying, do you? And in the process, you end up destroying the lives of people around you. People who genuinely love you and care for you!'

Manav's eyes welled up even as he tried to put up a brave front. Agni's gun was still trained on him.

'I think I know the answer, Mr Chauhan. You needed a *wife* to act as a cover for your secret double life. You thought that you would be able to masterfully *manage* a regular married life, like so many other closet gay men in our country. But, you've always been prey to the conflict between your loving heart and your thinking, calculating mind.'

'ACP Mitra, empathy doesn't sound convincing when you have a fucking gun in your hand!' Manav's eyes darted between Agni and Arya, as both of them aimed their guns at him.

Unfazed, Agni went on. 'You ended up breaking off your engagement with Neha with less than a month to go before your wedding. You could never bring yourself to marry her. You got cold feet at the last minute, but you didn't want to lose a family friend. That was a decision you made from your heart,' Agni inched closer to Manav. 'Within days, however, your mind took over. Hiya fell in love with you, and you didn't want to let the opportunity pass you by. But your relationship with Hiya turned sour soon after. It was the same story all over again. She missed the emotional connect. She missed intimacy. She found you cold and distant, because you had chosen her just as a prop in the grand story of your double life. Everyone close to her I spoke to – her colleagues, her secretary, the director of the movie she was acting in at that time – noticed the emotional turmoil she had been going through. It started affecting her work. And then, something rather extraordinary happened!'

'ACP, I admire your creativity! This is actually getting quite amusing now,' Manav tried to fake a smile. Rocky and Arya looked intently at Agni.

'Mayank and you took advantage of Hiya's emotional turmoil and engineered that *affair*. Infidelity would be a justifiable reason to break off your engagement with Hiya, won't it? Mr Chauhan, it makes me curious. Who were you listening to, on that occasion? Your heart, which was telling you to run away from the impending wedding and spare the poor girl? Or, was it Mayank, who was probably getting frustrated with your vacillating nature, and the uncertainties around his future with the man he was madly in love with? Was he pressurising you to break off your engagement, and come clean to the world about your relationship with him?'

Manav looked at Agni with unbelieving eyes. There was a storm brewing in his heart. He was suddenly consumed by hatred – hatred for himself, like always. He felt sorry for Hiya, all over again. He felt giddy. He leant back on the water tank, breathing heavily. Arya moved a few steps closer to Manav's side, holding on firmly to his gun.

Manav took his time to answer Agni's question. His face hidden in his palms, his body shook every now and then, as he failed to hold his tears back. 'It was Mayank's idea... it wasn't easy for him faking an affair with Hiya... but he did it for *us*...'

'And the plan almost worked. You enacted a very public spat with Mayank in a movie set, of all places! You turned Hiya's *infidelity* into a public spectacle and broke off your engagement with her. But, the girl was hopelessly in love with you. She realized her *mistake,* apologised and came back to you. You gave in, too. After all, that wedding *was* all that you had wanted in the first place. But, Mayank's brilliant plan had gone haywire with your marriage.'

Chapter 55

The beats from the party at Vibe had stopped. The wind roared on the roof, as yet another chilly night descended on the city. Sirens bellowed at a distance. The police cars were on their way. Agni's wait was almost over.

'Once you were married, it probably started getting increasingly difficult for you to manage your double life, with Mayank's impatience and his demands on your time and attention mounting by the day. Hiya was probably dangerously close to finding out about your secret life, too.'

Manav felt his stomach churning. The detective was playing out the darkest memories of his life, right in front of his eyes. Memories he had been trying for months to run away from. He wanted Agni to stop right there before he went on any further. But there was no stopping Agni that night, it seemed. It was the detective's way of overpowering him, worse than the battering Manav had received on his body a while back. From Rocky, who was kneeling on the floor in silence. Rocky loved Mayank, as much as Manav himself did. There was no way one could *not* fall in love with Mayank.

'That's when you scripted Hiya's *accidental* murder, Mr Chauhan. That would finally get her out of your way. You probably thought that bereavement would be an easier act for you than having to play the devoted husband at home and outside for the rest of your life! With Hiya gone, your secret would also be safe. Lastly, losing your new wife in a ghastly mishap would serve as a perfectly plausible psychological block against your willingness to get married to another woman ever again. Someone must have convinced you with that idea. Who was it? Mayank? Or, was it you, yourself?

'Lakhan, your trusted chauffeur who had been working with you for more than five years, knew Asif bhai and approached him. Asif bhai picked up the contract, engaged his boys who had a history of misdemeanour at Tipple, and took refuge abroad. You probably wanted him to stay in hiding till the dust had settled on the case.'

Manav tried hard to feign ridicule, and the effort showed.

'On that night, you enacted a public brawl with the three ruffians at Tipple, making sure that there were enough witnesses to put the blame on the three for everything that was going to happen to Hiya *and you* afterwards. When I spoke to Kuldeep Singh, the manager at Tipple, he mentioned that Hiya and you had not been regulars in that club. What that meant was that the staged brawl had been planned by someone close to you, someone who had known that you would land up at Tipple with your wife that night. I realized that no one would know your plans better than *you yourself,* Mr Chauhan! That staged brawl had been your brainchild all along.

When the two of you left Tipple, Lakhan drove the car to a desolate part of the town, instead of taking a busier alternate route. The hired goons had been following your car. When you reached the lonely New Town roads, they intercepted your car. You took a few blows yourself. So did Lakhan. The goons raped Hiya, before she was murdered. The rape would also ward off all suspicions of a pre-planned murder. Love does, often, bring out the beast inside us, doesn't it? You could go to any length for Mayank!'

Chapter 56

Manav closed his eyes. Images flashed in his mind – him writhing in pain on the dusty road, the three men dragging Hiya to a shed like a rag doll, their car at a distance. When Manav opened his eyes and looked up at Agni, his eyes were red and his face was contorted in pain. And it was not just the pain he felt all over his body.

The detective continued.

'You took good care of Lakhan and his family. You saw him off with a hefty sum of money. Probably fixed him up yourself with the Awasthis. That way, you made sure that your accomplice was removed from the household, yet did not go entirely out of your radar, if he ever decided to act smart. Lakhan paid off his debts, left the slum and moved with his family to a rented house. But destiny had other plans. Lakhan had tasted blood. He started blackmailing you. You coughed up money for a couple of months. All along, you kept in touch with Lakhan using a mobile phone number that could not be traced back to you. Then you realized that you had had enough and that it was not just about the money. Lakhan himself posed a threat. After all, he was the one who had engaged Asif bhai for you and had driven you to the location of the crime that night. What if he started talking? So you struck again. Who did you hire this time, Mr Chauhan?'

Manav did not answer. After a few seconds, he closed his eyes and whispered under his breath, '*Who would have imagined that old bugger had so much blood in him?* That was what he said... the man who killed Lakhan...'

Chapter 57

The sirens were not so distant anymore. Manav's heart pounded so hard he could hear it.

Agni continued, 'You know, Mr Chauhan, when I reconstructed this story, I was stuck at this point. When I met Mayank for the first time at The Nook after Hiya's death, he looked hurt, distraught, uncertain. And I asked myself why. If the sequence of events had indeed been like I narrate now, why was he depressed when there was no threat to his relationship with you anymore after Hiya's death? And then I found the answer. He was disoriented all over again, because of your growing proximity to Neha.

When I spoke to Neha, I realized she was ready to forgive you and forget everything she had gone through a few months back. She was contemplating a future with you. And you, Mr Chauhan, even after Hiya's death, refused to acknowledge before the world your feelings for Mayank. He found that humiliating. He had probably reached the limits of endurance. After all, this was the relationship for which Mayank was ready to put everything at stake. You, on the other hand, were desperate to hide your relationship with him, even using a fake identity for the mobile number you used to stay in touch with him. Yes, Mr Chauhan! In addition to the numbers of Rocky and Rituja, there is a third number that features prominently in Mayank's call records – one that we found out had been procured with fake identity proofs.'

188 | Sourabh Mukherjee

'He was being absolutely unreasonable!' Manav blurted out, finally opening up his buried chambers of pain. 'He was no longer the man I had fallen in love with, the man who I had wanted to spend the rest of my life with, the man in whose arms I used to find solace! I could not just pack my bags and leave my business here overnight! And I could not possibly stand on a fucking podium and declare my love for him, could I? But he refused to see sense! He was fucking blind!' Manav gasped for breath, as his outburst exhausted him. 'We fought every day. He started threatening me, said he would expose me. Started talking about his contacts in the television channels and the press...'

'And how could you let that happen, Mr Chauhan? You've always been the man in control. You've carefully handled your double life for years. There was no way you could throw all of that away at the whims of an irrational lover! In fact, you had, as usual, a change of mind and you were getting ready to marry Neha, having reconciled with the Awasthis. The wedding must be round the corner, right? Deepak Awasthi even got a plush restaurant set up in your mall that you inaugurated! Who knows? Maybe there are more in the pipeline! Which is good news for *his* business as well. Mayank was now a threat for you, perhaps the biggest you had encountered all these years!'

Agni's words and their ominous implication sent a chill down Rocky's spine, whose eyes were fixed on Manav, spewing venom.

'You pacified Mayank by talking about a beautiful life in a more liberal society. You promised to him that you would give up your empire here and move to London with him. Maybe you yourself wanted the same too, during fleeting moments of weakness when you were closer to your soul than your scheming, plotting mind. Mayank believed you. He was ready to throw away his career here – for you, for a future he had only dreamt of. He worked in confidence with Preeti and crafted a plan for the two of you flying out of Kolkata for London. The day before he died,

Preeti informed him that the tickets and travel documents for the two of you were ready. Rituja and he talked about this at Tipple. He wanted to tell Rocky when they met the next morning.

But you, Mr Chauhan, had other plans. You left the inauguration of the new restaurant in this mall and went to Galaxy. Doesn't take long from here, does it? About fifteen or twenty minutes at that hour of the night? You already had the key to the main gate at Galaxy. You've been one of Mayank's regular visitors in his flat, as we found out from the visitors' register. You walked in unnoticed when the security guard was away.

You took the elevator to Mayank's flat. Mayank was only too happy to see you and let you in. And then, things turned nasty. Mr Samaddar, Mayank's neighbour, heard him cry and shout before...'

Manav raised a hand, tears flowing down his blood-stained face. His temples throbbed in pain. He coughed out the bile.

'Please, ACP, please...'

'I won't continue, Mr Chauhan, if it pains you to remember your heinous act. But I have to say, it was clever of you to sneak out with Mayank's gadgets, making sure no one had access to any incriminating photos, messages, writings – for that matter, anything that would have revealed your secret love life...'

Manav rubbed his eyes with the back of his hand. The chill in the air further exacerbated his laboured breathing. He looked at Agni and spoke through his clenched teeth. 'You tied everything up nicely, ACP. Just as you had promised. But do you even have any evidence? Your story will sound compelling in a class of psychology, but I doubt if it will pass muster in a court of law unless you have evidence to back it up.' His words sounded more like his desperate attempt at figuring out the severity of the problems that stared him in the face, rather than the arrogant challenge that he had meant them to sound like.

'This is what brings down the sharpest of criminals, Mr Chauhan. Narcissism. God complex. This belief that one is a genius in a world infested with idiots!' Agni smiled, 'Mayank's friends – Rocky, Rituja – are ready to testify in a court of law. Mayank had told them that he was going to leave the country with his lover and your name is in the travel documents which Preeti has handed over to us. You managed to leave your fingerprints all over Mayank's flat. We'll now have a match right away. I've already got a search warrant issued for your houses to track down Mayank's gadgets. I'm sure you wouldn't have risked disposing of them. Who knows? Maybe the search will throw up the duplicate key to Galaxy as well, if we are lucky. You sure knew your way around Galaxy, Mr Chauhan. You visited Mayank in his flat eleven times in the last two months. We figured that out from our scrutiny of the visitor book at Galaxy, which presently is with us. And here comes the clincher, Mr Chauhan. Interpol has tracked Asif bhai down in Dubai. We have already sought response to an extradition request through the office of Foreign Ministry. The repatriation would be an easy process as the two countries have an extradition treaty. And from what I've heard, Asif bhai is ready to sing!'

Chapter 58

Manav's face had a deathly pallor.

The sirens were heard downstairs. Agni knew there were armed policemen streaming out of the police cars and running towards the entrance of the mall that very moment. Agni looked at his watch. Exactly the time Agni had wanted them to be there, when he had spoken to the officer in-charge over phone immediately after reaching Vibe with Arya. Of course, he had not foreseen the events that had unfolded over the last half an hour on the roof of the Town Centre Mall.

'ACP, why don't you finish off this... this mess of a life?' Manav screamed in agony as he straightened up gingerly and tottered towards Agni's gun. 'I am tired running from myself!'

'I don't give in to provocation, Mr Chauhan. You've blood in your hands. You are responsible for three murders... two of your victims were madly in love with you. I'm not going to let you die a hero's death here. You deserve to rot in jail!'

'Love? You talk of love? Ever lived in fear of being an outcast because you are in love?'

'Mr Chauhan, I could fight for your rights till the last day of my life. For everyone like you. But I will never stand by a murderer!'

Agni could hear heavy footsteps on the stairs. Almost at the same moment, there was a movement he noticed from the corner of his eye.

It was Rocky. He stood up and made a dash for Manav, his insane rage suddenly getting the better of him. Like Manav himself, Rocky did not want him to land up in jail. He had to get to him before the police did. He had his own reasons.

'Rocky, I tell you again, get a hold on yourself!' Agni cried as he turned his gun on him. Arya had swivelled in his direction as well.

Out of the line of fire of both, Manav gathered the last vestiges of his energy and made a dash for the edge of the roof.

Before Rocky managed to pounce on his prey, before Arya had the time to close the distance, before Agni's shot missed his right foot, Manav Chauhan had jumped into the night.

Chapter 59

Manav Chauhan

I can hear sirens below as I fall through the chilly air of the night.

Sirens. I have always been afraid of them. Whenever I went out with Mayank and returned late in the night in hired cabs instead of my own cars, the sirens of police patrol cars would scare me. So much that I would hastily take my hand off his and make sure we did not sit too close to each other. Because the society and the law had no name for our relationship. And when you do not have a name for a relationship, you conveniently end up calling it immoral, illegal and even 'unnatural'. The police would only be too happy to harass us and cash in on our vulnerability and fear to make a fast buck.

When one is destined to walk down a path less trodden, one is likely to face roadblocks galore – self-doubt, resistance from the family and aspersions of the society in general. All that people have are weird looks and hushed whispers. I remembered the time when I had gone out shopping with a boy when I was in college. We happened to hold hands. I threw caution to the wind and in a careless moment, I knelt against him as we came down an escalator in the shopping mall. A security staff in the mall approached us and asked us to 'behave'. Later that evening in a café, when my friend put an arm around me, we were warned that it was a 'family café'! Of course, there was no way that the two of us could dream of ever being 'family'! The world taught me my lessons, quick and early.

The proof of our inner strength lies not in making choices that could invite the sneer and the wrath of the society, but in seeing those choices through. If we believe in the choices we make for ourselves, like I chose Mayank, none of these resistances should really matter. I am a staunch believer in this philosophy. And going by this yardstick, I know that I am definitely not strong. No doubt about that.

Because my mind and my heart, if they can indeed be called apart, are always in conflict. The ACP was right!

There is a part of me that is ever willing to surrender everything at the altar of love. To fight traditions and customs that get in the way. To hold on to my love like it was my life itself and never let it go.

And then, there is a part of me that fears ridicule, that cannot handle rejection, that seeks validation. I realized early in my life that the only way to gain acceptance was to conform to hackneyed customs, to outdated norms in what we proudly claim to be a progressive society. All these at the cost of my feelings, and the tears I shed in the solitude of my room every night.

I remembered how Mayank and I celebrated after I broke off my engagement with Neha citing our differences. I remembered how happy Mayank was when his plan worked and I broke off my engagement with Hiya, accusing her of adultery. We went on a long drive, we were together all night, lost in each other, in our own world where all that mattered was our love for each other, as true and as pure as the holy books. We got drunk, we made love, we even decided what we would call the babies we would raise together. Doesn't every human being in love do that? So, what makes us 'different'?

But guess what? I am just not strong enough. And I hate myself for that, more than I hate the world around me. Because if I fail to *stand up for myself, why blame the world? The rebel in me wakes up time and again and seeks justice for my tears. But I fail every time. I fail because there is a part of me that seeks acceptance. And the society we live in demands too high a price for it.*

Does my weakness make me insincere in my love? Should you not love, if you lack the strength to take on the world for the sake of your love? And why does the world have to mercilessly crush under its unforgiving heels any kind of love that it fails to find a name for?

I do not have answers to these questions. I never did. And murder is often the easiest resort for the weak. For the escapist. For people like me.

Mayank called me the night I was released from the hospital. He did not understand why I did not sound 'like the way I always did', as he put it. That was because I was sad. I was sad for Hiya. I was sorry for what I had done. I cared for that girl. As a human being, if not as a lover or a husband. She loved me. She trusted me.

But Mayank had changed. He did not understand me anymore. I guess love does that to you. It makes you unreasonably possessive. It makes you blind.

I remember the night I met him last in his flat.

I went to his flat that night and broke the news. I had decided to marry Neha. The date was a couple of weeks away. I did not have the courage to stand before the world and make my relationship with Mayank public. I could not run away from my carefully etched life of lies and land up in faraway London with him.

That was the only reason why I went to see Mayank that night. I had no idea how the night would end.

I assured Mayank that my marriage to Neha would not change anything. Nothing could change the way I felt for Mayank. We would still be together.

'Since when did you start bothering about a name for our relationship?' I asked him. 'Isn't it enough that I love you more than anyone or anything else in this world? I'll always be yours Mayank,

I promise!' I pleaded with him. Somewhere deep inside, I wanted him to agree to the arrangement. Nothing was more important to me at that moment.

He was drunk. He had been out drinking all evening with that heroine of his, Rituja. He was drinking when I reached his flat. He did not listen to me.

'Manav, weren't we supposed to fly out of this country? Weren't we supposed to go where we could breathe freely? Weren't we supposed to go where we wouldn't have to be scared of the sirens and the flashing lights of the patrol cars? What happened to your promises? What happened to my dreams?' Mayank cried inconsolably. He cried so much that he was soon out of breath. He could barely stand straight. Drool dripped past his mouth. He began to curse the mother who had given birth to him. He kept saying that he was cursed being born the way he was.

'Why are you doing this to me, Manav? You've no idea what I've been going through for months! For god's sake, when will you take a stand for us? For our love?' Mayank wailed, in between his helpless gasps. 'We have everything sorted out now. The travel documents have arrived. I'll collect them tomorrow. And then, we can be free. Forever!'

I could not hold back my own tears. I loved him. I could not see him cry. But he would not listen to reason.

We were in his bedroom. I wanted to take him in my arms so that he could feel my heart beating only for him. I wanted to silence him by taking his lips between mine.

But Mayank started threatening me.

'Manav, do you want me to call Neha right now?'

'Manav, do you want me to call your dad?'

'Manav, be honest at least to yourself...'

'Manav, do you even love me?'

'Manav, you could've told me you were just looking for some fun on the side and I'd have played along... I've had friends with benefits

all my life before you came along... why the fuck did you make me dream of a family, for god's sake? Do you even know what it's like to dream?'

Mayank was choking on his words. And he was scaring me.

'Mayank, you've suffered enough. You fell in love with the wrong man...' I said, hugging him tight.

My lips landed on his. I tried to kiss him.

He freed himself, pushing me away.

'I can't see you suffer like this,' I whispered. 'You need to sleep, dear! You've suffered enough!' I repeated.

By now, we were in the bedroom balcony and Mayank was dangerously close to the edge.

'I'm not going to let you get away with this, Manav! I'm not going to let you fuck with my life...' he shouted into the cold, silent night.

I felt sorry for the man I loved. I could not see him suffer the way he did. I felt sorry for the love I lived for. Because I was not strong enough to stand by it, which made my beloved doubt the honesty of my feelings for him. At the same time, I was in the grip of fear. I could see my carefully crafted plan crashing in front of my eyes. My conflicting emotions cast a spell on me and numbed my senses. Mayank was going on and on, his voice seemed to be floating in from another world, his face shrouded by his unruly hair was like a dark ominous haze.

In a split second, I pushed him. Off the edge of that balcony. I watched him fall to sleep, to eternal peace that his tormented soul demanded.

But destiny had its own plans.

I never imagined we would be united so soon, our journey to eternal bliss unfolding just as Mayank had planned it. He would leave first, and I would follow. I can see my love waiting for me – his messy locks all over his face, his lips curved in that lopsided smile that never failed to make my heart skip a beat, his arms stretched for me. Just for me!

As the sirens grow louder, I can feel his arms closing around me, his lips seeking mine. Mayank must have forgiven me.